DS.

SPECIAL MESSAGE TO READERS

THE ULVERSCROFT FOUNDATION
(registered UK charity number 264873)
was established in 1972 to provide funds for
research, diagnosis and treatment of eye diseases.
Examples of major projects funded by
the Ulverscroft Foundation are:-

- The Children's Eye Unit at Moorfields Eye Hospital, London
- The Ulverscroft Children's Eye Unit at Great Ormond Street Hospital for Sick Children
- Funding research into eye diseases and treatment at the Department of Ophthalmology, University of Leicester
- The Ulverscroft Vision Research Group, Institute of Child Health
- Twin operating theatres at the Western Ophthalmic Hospital, London
- The Chair of Ophthalmology at the Royal Australian College of Ophthalmologists

You can help further the work of the Foundation
by making a donation or leaving a legacy.
Every contribution is gratefully received. If you
would like to help support the Foundation or
require further information, please contact:

THE ULVERSCROFT FOUNDATION
The Green, Bradgate Road, Anstey
Leicester LE7 7FU, England
Tel: (0116) 236 4325

website: www.foundation.ulverscroft.com

MYSTERY AT CASA LARGO

When Samantha Davis is made redundant, she turns to her boy-friend Steve for consolation — only to discover he is cheating on her. With both job and relationship having vanished in the space of one day, she feels left on the scrapheap, until her mother suggests she travel to Portugal to work at her friend Georgina's guesthouse. There, she meets Georgina's attractive son, Hugo — and the mysterious, taci-turn Simon . . .

MIRANDA BARNES

MYSTERY AT CASA LARGO

Complete and Unabridged

LINFORD
Leicester

First published in Great Britain in 2014

First Linford Edition
published 2016

A catalogue record for this book is available
from the British Library.

ISBN 978–1–4448–2692–0

1

'Samantha Davis, please!'

Sam stood up and brushed biscuit crumbs off her skirt.

'Good luck, Sam!' Lisa whispered.

'Luck? I need more than that, I think.'

She smiled at her friend and turned to follow the man in the doorway. It was like a hospital waiting room, she couldn't help thinking. Everybody wanting to know their fate, and to learn if they had any future.

'You can always emigrate!' Colin called to her. 'Australia's nice at this time of year, I believe.'

'It might very well come to that,' she said, chuckling.

The man waiting for her smiled, as if he too appreciated the joke, and the situation. 'You've all been here a long time, I suppose?' he said.

1

'Six or seven years in my case, but some — like Colin there — have been here a lot longer than that.'

The young man grimaced and ushered her along the corridor. 'I'm Jack, by the way,' he said as they walked along.

She nodded, thinking he seemed a bit young to have much responsibility in the current situation. But perhaps accountants working for receivers were young. It would be a tough job, coping with people's fears and anxieties — and their anger as well, no doubt.

But Jack turned out to be no more than an usher. He showed her into an office where a man and a woman, both middle-aged, weary-looking people, sat behind a long table. They had her sit down, too, apologised for the lack of coffee facilities — unpaid bills and no cash in the till, apparently — and got straight on with it.

They had, the woman said not quite apologetically, a large number of people to see today. So Sam would understand if they got straight down to business?

Sam nodded, smiled politely and waited to be told if there was a job for her still.

No, it seemed. There wasn't. That news was delivered even more quickly than she had anticipated.

'We really are terribly sorry to have to tell you this, Miss Davis,' the man said, 'but we're afraid there's nothing here for you. In fact, there's nothing much here for anybody. All we are doing is trying to pick up the pieces and clear up the mess.'

Sam was stung by his curt delivery of such an unwelcome message. 'I understand the problem, Mr . . . I'm sorry. I didn't catch your name?'

'Richardson, Jack Richardson, of Peake and O'Toole. My colleague is Mrs Helen Smythe. The two of us have been appointed the official receivers for the company.'

Sam nodded. Official receivers? Whatever they were. The situation was obviously bad, worse even than she had understood.

She tried again. 'Mr Richardson, I understand that the business — the company — is in trouble. Of course I do. Big trouble. I work in Accounts, and we've all heard that things have not been going well lately.

'All the same, it is a big business — and a big factory. There's all the equipment, the stocks, the materials — and so many highly-skilled people. We have lots of orders, as well, I understand. Quality rugs and carpets have been made here for over a hundred years! Is there really nothing left for any of us to do?'

'Not much,' Mr Richardson said grimly, shaking his head. 'The business has run into the buffers, I'm afraid. Initially, we had hoped to find a buyer for it, but now we've realised that's impossible.

'We'll simply liquidate the business, and sell off what we can. Plant, equipment and so on. Whatever monies we raise will go to the principal creditor, HMG. There will be nothing left to pay any of the other creditors.'

He glanced meaningfully at his watch but Sam wasn't prepared to let it go quite yet. MacDonald & Flanagan Ltd. had been a large part of her life these past few years. Besides, there were people with families to feed and mortgages to pay, people far worse off than her. She was thinking of them, too.

'Presumably you will need staff to run things while you . . . '

'Miss Davis,' Mrs Smythe intervened, 'we do appreciate how difficult this is for you to accept. But the truth is that the business has become an empty shell. You must reconcile yourself to looking for a job elsewhere, I'm afraid.

'In the meantime, of course, you will qualify for the usual statutory benefits, and for assistance in job hunting. The local Job Centre . . . '

'So I'm on the dole, or whatever it's called now, am I?' Sam asked, suddenly and annoyingly close to tears.

Mrs Smythe nodded. 'I'm sorry,' she said.

And that was that.

★　★　★

Afterwards, she left and set off for home. There was nothing here for her any more. A mid-week work day, and she was not at work. How could it be?

She shook her head. It was a mystery to her. How could such a sensible old company, that made highly-regarded, good-quality products, end up in such a shambles? It was beyond her. Everything had seemed perfectly normal until a week or two ago, when the rumours started to fly and important people started holding meetings that had not been scheduled.

Oh, well. That's how it is, she concluded. Nothing I can do, say or think will make it any better. I'm just going to have to get on with it. At least I don't have a family dependent on me.

I'll manage, and I'll find another job somewhere.

That's it, she thought grimly. I'm drawing a line under the whole thing. Today is the start of the rest of my life.

★ ★ ★

Instead of continuing on home, she changed her mind and headed for Gosforth to see Steve. It was half-term, which meant he wouldn't be working today either. They could do something nice together, and try to enjoy themselves. No need to spend it feeling sorry for herself.

That was one thing about Steve, she thought warmly. He might, as he said himself, be a boring old teacher, but he was such good fun. He could always bring a smile to her face. Why, even now, just thinking about him she was beginning to smile. She couldn't wait to tell him what had happened, and to be lovingly consoled, before making the most of an unexpected free day.

But that was as good as her day got. With the advantage of hindsight, she wished she had just taken her troubles home, talked to Mum and started job hunting.

Steve wasn't at work, of course. She was right about that. And he was at home in his posh flat. She had got that right, too. It was a possibility she had never even considered that contrived to make her day even worse than it had already been.

A pretty young woman Sam had never seen before came to the door. She was wearing a bathrobe over not very much else. Sam stared, stunned.

'Oh, hello!' the woman said. 'Have you come for your parcel? Steve said they left it here. I'll just ask him where it is.'

'No, I . . .'

'Come in!' the woman insisted. 'I'll ask him where he put it. Don't mind me being dressed like this. We haven't been up long.'

Sam shook her head. Face burning, her insides churning, she turned to walk away.

'Is something wrong?' the woman called after her.

'No, nothing at all,' she said over her shoulder. 'Just tell Steve that Sam called, will you?'

2

Shock gave way to anger, and even rage, as she walked away. Of all the . . . She couldn't believe what she had just seen and been forced to accept. How could he? How dare he! Steve, of all people.

She didn't bother with the bus or the metro. She walked. She tried to walk it out of her system. The last thing she wanted was to sit in close proximity to scores of people she didn't know, all probably wondering what had got into this woman who seemed to oscillate between tears and rage. Better to keep to herself until she calmed down.

So she walked all the way back to Fenham. It took her an hour. By the time she got there rage and anger had faded. Now she just felt abject misery. This should not have happened. It really shouldn't. She had trusted Steve implicitly. She had been prepared to start thinking about a long-term future with him. Perhaps even more. A family. A home. Permanence. Now it was all gone, all that hope and expectation. Now she had nothing, nothing at all. Neither a job nor a boyfriend, and so far as she could see no future either. She was left on the scrapheap. Her life was the absolute pits!

It was just as well the house was empty when she arrived. She opened the door, stepped inside and paused to listen. Nothing. Good, she thought with relief. Dad was at work, and Mum must be out at the shops. Or . . . What day was it? Tuesday. Maybe she was visiting someone. Shopping was done on Monday, and then again on Thursday or Friday. Today she would be visiting. Mum had her routines, just as she herself had had until today.

She climbed the stairs wearily and retreated to her room, to flop on her back on the bed. Oh, Steve! She turned over and buried her face in the pillow for a few moments to staunch the tears.

The bad moment passed. Eventually she sat up and decided to take a shower. The long walk had left her feeling hot and dirty. The city's grit and dust had coated her arms and face, and her hair felt and smelled unpleasant.

As she undressed, she wondered if Steve would phone and try to explain what had happened, and apologise profusely. It didn't matter if he did or he didn't, she decided. It was over. She would never be able to trust him again. He wasn't the man she had thought he was, and he wasn't the man she wanted in her life any more. It was over.

★　★　★

'Hello? Is that you, Samantha?' Mum called up the stairs in a rather timid voice.

'Yes, it is! Hello, Mum.'

'That's all right, then. I wondered if we had a burglar.'

Sam gave a wry smile and shook her

12

head. 'I'll be down in a minute, Mum.'

Burglars would have slim pickings in this house, she thought ruefully. What would they find? My P45, or whatever it was called?

Stop it! she said sternly. Just stop feeling sorry for yourself. That's not going to help anybody.

'There you are!' Mum said as she arrived in the kitchen.

Then she peered closer, inspecting her, and said, 'Are you all right, love? What are you doing here at this time of day? Not ill, are you?'

'Am I all right?' Sam said with a wry chuckle and a rueful smile. 'I've seldom been worse, actually.'

'Why? Whatever's the matter? Are you feeling off colour?'

'Oh, I'm all right in that sense. Not in others, though. It's been one of those mornings, I'm afraid.'

'Has it? Well, sit down, and tell me about it. I've just made a pot of tea, but I've put two tea bags in. I'm not used to seeing you here at this time of day,' she added. 'On a weekday, as well.'

'Well, you're going to have to get used to it, Mum. For a little while, at least. I just hope it won't be for too long.'

★ ★ ★

'And is there no hope?' Mum asked, when Sam had finished telling her about her meeting with the receivers.

'None at all. They were quite clear about that. They don't even want people to help sell stuff off for them. Fixtures and fittings, and what have you. I think they'll just send the bulldozers in and flatten the whole place.'

'Oh, dear. How dreadful. I wonder what the family will think. It must be awful for them.'

'If the family had done a better job of running the business, instead of swanning off around the world at every opportunity, maybe it wouldn't have come to this!

'I'm talking about the current owners, of course, not the previous generation. This last lot are just playboys and girls, from what I can make out about them.'

'Oh dear. Are they really?'

'Anyway,' Sam added more quietly, 'it's not them I'm thinking about. It's all the poor people who have families to feed, and mortgages to pay. All the people who have worked so long and hard for the company. They didn't deserve this.'

'Neither did you, Sam. Don't forget that. You've been there a long time, and you've worked hard, too.'

Sam rolled her eyes and sighed. She wasn't good at thinking much about herself.

'What will you do, love?'

'I have no idea, Mum. They told me to visit the Job Centre. I suppose I'd better do that straight away, but I'm not keen.'

'You'll soon find something else. With all your experience and qualifications, I know you will.'

Sam didn't know about that. She was glad to have the support, but she knew it wasn't going to be easy. You heard so much about how difficult it was to find a job these days. Even if you were prepared to work for the minimum wage, jobs still seemed to be very hard to find.

'I tell you what, though, Mum,' she said spiritedly. 'I'm not going to just rush into the first thing I see. I'm going to find something I really like, and really want to do. I don't want to go to work feeling miserable every day — if I can find a job at all, that is.'

Mum nodded. 'More tea, dear?'

'I suppose so.' She yawned and added, 'Why not?'

'Why don't you talk to Steve about it?' Mum asked. 'I keep hearing about all these special programmes for people who want to retrain as teachers. Maybe you could try something like that? Steve should be able to advise you.'

'Steve?' Sam gave a bitter little laugh. 'Talk to him is the last thing I'll do now.

I haven't told you yet about what else happened this morning, have I?'

'Oh, dear! What's happened now? Have you two fallen out?'

*   *   *

'That's scandalous!' Mum exclaimed after Sam had told what she had discovered.

'No, Mum. It's just how some people live these days. Not me, but there's plenty who would think it quite normal. Anyway, there's no law against it. I just didn't know Steve was like that.'

'So what are you going to do — have it out with him?'

Sam shook her head. 'It's over. I don't want to see or talk to Steve ever again. He's in my past — just like my old job!'

3

Finding a new job really wasn't easy. In one sense, that didn't surprise her. It was what she had expected. But the mechanics of looking and searching were even more dispiriting than she had anticipated. The endless poring over newspapers, and the online files of vacancies at the Job Centre. The endless internet searches. It was hard to spot anything at all for which she seemed remotely qualified. Then there was the question of what she actually wanted to do. For that, she had no answer. She simply believed, and hoped, that she would know it when she saw it — if it ever appeared.

Dad didn't help, counselling patience and optimism with his own, at times infuriatingly, endless optimism.

'Oh, Dad!' she complained. 'You have no idea what it's like these days.'

'That's true,' he admitted with a grin. 'In my day, jobs were two a penny. You could be anything you wanted — coal miner, brain surgeon, blacksmith, professor of engineering at the university. All you had to do was toss a coin to see which way your future lay.'

'Very funny,' she said with a scowl, swatting him with a rolled newspaper to stop him laughing. 'That's quite enough of that, thank you very much.'

'Something will turn up, love,' he assured her. 'Just you see.'

She grimaced and said she was beginning to doubt it.

★ ★ ★

Steve phoned, full of bluster and blarney, and self-justification. She wasn't interested in any of it, and told him so bluntly.

'You can't let a little thing like that bother you!' he protested. 'I made a mistake. That's all. It won't happen again. People who . . . '

19

'You've got the wrong person, Steve, if you think something like that is not something to get worked up about. And I had the wrong man. Forget it. Move on, like I'm doing. Goodbye!'

He had some nerve trying to explain it away, she thought indignantly. Having another woman in his flat might not seem of much significance to him, but it certainly did to her. Forget it, buddy!

For a few minutes she stomped around feeling fully charged and better about herself. No-one was walking all over her! Then she turned back to practical matters, and the job hunt, and the day lost its sparkle once again.

⋆　⋆　⋆

That evening Mum made an irritating suggestion that didn't help at all. If anything, it made her feel even worse. It started in a kindly way, though. As always, Mum was well intentioned.

'You seem very out of sorts, pet.'

'That's not altogether surprising, is

it?' Sam said with a yawn.

'Well, it's not like you.'

Much more of this, Sam thought wearily, and I'll be really fed up. I'll probably say something I'm sorry about afterwards. I've had three weeks of sitting at home and job hunting. I've about had enough. No wonder people get depression when they're out of work for a long time.

'Have you thought of branching out and doing something totally different?' Mum persisted.

'Like what?'

'Oh, I don't know. Anything, really.'

'What have you got in mind?' Sam asked, sensing there was something tangible behind this diplomatic approach. 'What are you thinking?'

'Oh, nothing really.'

'Mum! I know you. You can't fool me. What is it? Tell me.'

Mum sighed and put aside the cardigan she had been mending.

'Well, it just so happens that I had a letter recently from an old friend who moved to Portugal many years ago. Georgina Conway. I don't know if you remember her? You probably don't, actually. You were much too young at the time. Anyway, she runs a guest-house there, in the Algarve.'

'Oh, Mum!' Sam said with irritation. 'The last thing I need is a holiday. Anyway, I can't afford one. I've got to look after what little money I have. It might have to last me a long time.'

'It's a very nice place, apparently. A nice area, too. Dad and I went to the Algarve once, just before you were born,' Mum continued, as if Sam had not spoken. 'There were olive trees everywhere. And it was lovely and hot. I remember that very well. Once it was so hot that . . . '

'Mum! I've told you. I don't want a holiday.'

'I wasn't thinking of a holiday, darling. That's not why I mentioned it, not at all. I was thinking about a job. Georgina said she could do with some help for the season.'

'Oh, Mum! What are you like? Portugal must be absolutely full of young, unemployed people desperate to find work. Their economy is worse than ours, from what I hear on the news.'

'I'm sure you're right, dear. But what Georgina says she wants — and needs — is someone from this country to help her. Most of her guests are British, you see. And they want to be able to talk to someone in their own language.'

'Well, it's not me she needs,' Sam said firmly. 'And that's not what I want either,' she added even more firmly.

'No?' Mum said with a disappointed sigh. 'What a pity. Oh, well. I did try.'

4

Most of the way there Sam felt sick and full of dread. What was she doing? What on earth had possessed her? Surely things hadn't been that bad?

But they had. She knew that really. She had needed very much to get away from home for a while. Mum had known that, too, bless her.

So here she was, on her way. Ready to give it a try. Anything seemed better than sitting at home, brooding, waiting for a job offer that never came.

Besides, Georgina had been very nice when she spoke to her on the phone. In fact, she had seemed desperate for her to go. It was always nice when you were wanted, Sam thought with a rueful smile. You couldn't beat being wanted!

This was going to work, she told herself firmly. She had needed something, preferably something different to what she was used to. Now she had it. She was determined to make the most of the opportunity, and to see where it led.

★ ★ ★

The plane slid out of the clouds and the world below was suddenly bathed in sunshine. It was a stunning transformation and her mood changed as she watched the dry, scrub-covered hills appear and then give way to the lagoons and sand bars along the coast.

Oh my! It was so beautiful. She held her breath with awe.

The plane juddered as it hit an air bubble and she gave an involuntary little shiver. Then the plane banked, and all she could see for a few moments was the deep blue of the endless sea as they turned in a leisurely arc to run along the coast to Faro.

The Algarve!

She wondered again what it would be

like, and what awaited her at Casa
Largo.

* * *

Georgina was waiting for her when she
emerged from Arrivals into the searing
brightness and blistering white heat.
Sam had wondered if they would
recognise each other, but they did
instantly. Georgina was the one with
curly red hair and a cheery smile, and
she was waving frantically.

'Sam, you made it!'

'Hello, Georgina.'

Sam smiled with relief.

'Welcome to the Algarve!'

'Thank you. It's lovely to be here.'

They hugged one another and
Georgina gave Sam a peck on the
cheek.

'How are your mum and dad?'

'Fine, thank you. Mum wanted to
come with me, I think.'

'She should have!'

'Dad thought it might be too warm

for him, the old stick-in-the-mud! Anyway, it's lovely to see you, Georgina. I wondered if anybody would be here to meet me.'

'How could you have doubted it? Of course I would be here. I'm sure your mum would have said so.'

'Well, yes. She did, actually. All the same . . . Thank you again.'

Georgina stepped back and gazed at her. 'You look so well, Sam. It's wonderful to see you again after all this time. How long is it? Oh, my goodness! It's years. You were only little.'

'It's been quite a while, anyway,' Sam agreed with a smile, not sure she could even recall a previous meeting. 'It's good to see you, too — and good just to be here. I never thought it would really happen.'

Georgina laughed and made a grab for one of her bags. 'Come on! Your car is waiting.'

The car park was only a couple of minutes' walk away. Such a difference, Sam thought, to one of those vast airports where you needed a courtesy bus to take you to your car.

'How is everybody back home?' Georgina asked as they put Sam's case and bags in the boot of her car.

'Oh, you know. The same. Mum is still so busy, and Dad too. They're fine. Probably glad to get rid of me, actually. It's time they had the house to themselves for a while. They must have thought I would never leave home.'

'I'm sure that's not true. What a thing to say!'

'Well . . . ' Sam smiled and dried up, wanting the subject to be changed.

'And you?' Georgina said. 'You're quite well?'

'Me?' Sam laughed. 'Yes, of course I am. Why . . . ?'

'Nothing, nothing! Just an impression I had from your mum that you'd been under the weather a bit. That's all.'

It was true, Sam supposed. Under the weather was a nice old-fashioned way of putting it. So much gentler than having to admit to a failed relationship, and to all the heartache and anguish that accompanied that and being made redundant at the same time.

'Phew!' she said, fanning her face. 'It's so hot here. I can't believe it. Back home, it was still winter.'

'Hot?' Georgina said as she started the car. 'Not really. Not yet. Today it's still in the twenties. Just you wait a couple of months. Then the thermometer will start to climb.'

Sam wondered how badly she would wilt when that happened. She had never been a sun worshipper.

'But don't worry,' Georgina said cheerfully. 'You'll be acclimatised by then.'

'That's good to know. So what about Casa Largo? Are you busy already?'

'Oh, yes. Very. We've been pretty busy ever since January, actually.'

Georgina stopped the car to feed her ticket into the machine that lifted the barrier, allowing them to leave.

'I can't tell you,' she added as they set off again, 'how glad I am that you've come to give me a hand. I was so pleased when your mum first mentioned the possibility.'

Sam smiled. If things worked out well, she thought, they would be helping each other. That was better than thinking of herself as a charity case.

Georgina fiddled with the air conditioning controls until a blast of cold air emerged. 'There!' she said. 'That better?'

'Much, thank you,' Sam admitted.

* * *

They got going and soon left Faro behind as they ran inland towards the distant wooded hills. Lucy looked around eagerly at the unfamiliar landscape. On each side of the road were what seemed to be smallholdings, with patchwork fields, poly tunnels and a scatter of little traditional houses, many of them looking rather run-down.

'It's not exactly picture postcard

30

territory, is it?' Georgina said, noticing Sam's interest in their surroundings.

Sam smiled. 'Perhaps not, but it is interesting. Oh, look!'

'What?'

'Oranges — on trees!'

Georgina chuckled. 'You'll see plenty of them, my dear. Oranges, and lemons, too. You'll soon be sick of the sight of them. Sunshine, too, I shouldn't wonder. You'll be longing for rain and green grass.'

'Never! I don't believe that for one moment.'

'You'll see.'

One day, she might, Sam supposed. But it was hard to imagine, and it certainly wasn't going to happen for a while. This was all so wonderfully different.

'How long a drive is it?' she asked.

Georgina shrugged. 'Depending on the traffic, and whether there have been any accidents, twenty or thirty minutes. Not long. Why? Tired?'

'No. I just wondered. Sao Bras de

Alportel didn't look far on the map, but I didn't know how long it would take to get there.'

'We're just outside the town, actually. Casa Largo is in the hills a mile or two to the north. At one time it was a little farm, but then the people who owned it got tired of growing olives and turned to tourism instead.'

'Is it a big house?'

'Oh, no. It's not a vast villa, or anything like that. There's my little house. Then there's eight units for guests. We call them cottages, but they're really converted farm buildings. Small, but cosy.'

Sam nodded. 'Did you and Mike do the conversions?'

'No. All that was already done when we bought the place.'

Sam nodded and let the subject drop. She was sorry now that she had mentioned the name of Georgina's ex-husband. It had just popped out.

'Don't worry about it,' Georgina said.

'Pardon?'

'Me and Mike — or perhaps I should say Mike's absence. I'm used to it. We split up a long time ago. It's done with.'

Sam nodded. She was almost relieved that Georgina had picked up on her hesitation. It seemed to absolve her of guilt for mentioning Mike's name.

'It's just like you and wot's-'is-name,' Georgina added with a grin. 'We're both in the same boat really, aren't we?'

'Steve?' Sam had to laugh. 'Well, yes,' she admitted ruefully. 'Perhaps we are.'

Not quite, though, she thought. She and Steve had been a long way from being married, thank goodness.

'New life here we come!' Georgina added firmly.

Perhaps, Sam thought. She certainly hoped so.

'Oh, look!' she said, leaning forward. 'What are those men doing?'

Several men were working amongst the trees in a small copse. One or two were at a height. Others were parcelling up stacks of a strange grey-coloured material.

33

'They're stripping off the bark,' Georgina said, after a quick sideways glance.

'Whatever for?'

'For cork. Those are cork oak trees, and this is cork farming country.'

'Cork?'

'If you've ever wondered where all those funny little things that seal wine bottles come from . . . '

'Oh, cork!' Sam said, as the penny dropped. 'Really? Is this where it comes from?'

'Much of it,' Georgina said with a grin. 'Welcome to the old Algarve! The cork industry was here long before the tourists and us dropouts started coming.'

Us dropouts? Sam thought. Was that what they were? Was that what she was now? Perhaps it was, but she didn't like the sound of it. She, at least, hadn't dropped out. How she thought of it was that coming here was going to be the start of something new and good in her life. That was the plan, at least.

5

'Here we are,' Georgina said, turning the car off the tarmac and onto a gravel track. 'It's just up there.'

Sam peered through the windscreen at the group of buildings ahead, on top of a small hill. 'Oh, my!' she gasped. 'What a wonderful location.'

'Yes. We can see for miles.'

They trundled up the rough track and through the twin pillars that marked the entrance to the grounds of Casa Largo.

'It looks very grand,' Sam said as they drove along a short drive lined with stately palm trees that were dancing in a light breeze.

'It's falling to bits, though,' Georgina said.

Sam could tell she didn't really mean it, and that she was quietly pleased with Sam's reaction to her first sight of Casa Largo.

Georgina stopped the car and switched off the engine. 'Here we are,' she said with a bright smile. 'Home!'

They sat for a moment, giving Sam the chance to gaze all around her. She took in the lawns and the banks of gorgeous flowering shrubs, the pool shimmering in the sunlight, and the palm trees shivering and rustling in the welcome breeze. Beyond, partly hidden by leaves and flowers, there was a little clutter of white stone buildings with faded terracotta pantile roofs. It seemed perfect, a dream.

'Oh, Georgina,' she said softly. 'It's absolutely lovely.'

Her host smiled and opened her door. 'Come on,' she said. 'It's far too hot to sit here like this. I'll give you a quick tour. Then we'll find something cool to drink, and see about some lunch.'

As they were pulling Sam's luggage out of the boot, a young man walked up to them. He was tall and slim, and had a shock of black, curly hair. He seemed a little agitated but pleased to see them.

'There you are, Mum! I was worried about you.'

'Oh, Hugo!' Georgina replied, laughing and shaking her head. 'I did tell you what I was doing this morning. I've just been to the airport to collect Sam. Remember? She's going to be with us for a while. Sam, meet Hugo, my son.'

'Hello, Hugo! I'm pleased to meet you.'

'Hi.'

He gave her a shy smile, shook her outstretched hand and then turned to walk away without saying anything else at all.

Surprised, Sam glanced at Georgina, who just shrugged and said with a sigh, 'Come on. Let's go inside.'

* * *

The main house at Casa Largo was old and cool, dark inside with elaborately tiled floors and a hallway with tiles that climbed halfway up the walls. Sam looked around with fascination as Georgina led her through to the kitchen.

'What a lovely old fireplace,' she said, spotting the elaborately tiled hearth. 'Do you use it? Do you need it, in fact?'

'In winter we do. It can be chilly and damp when the rains come.'

Somehow that was hard to believe.

'Sit down, sit down!' Georgina urged. 'Let me get you some lemonade.'

It was real lemonade, too, Sam realised, as with delight she sipped what Georgina brought her. 'How lovely! Is it home-made? It can't be.'

'Yes, it is. I made it,' Georgina admitted. 'We have so many lemons on the trees around here that you have to do something with them. The oranges are not so bad. I make marmalade with them. But there's not so much you can do with lemons.'

Sam smiled and shook her head with admiration and envy. The very idea of having so many oranges and lemons that you struggled to know what to do with them was rather wonderful, as well as intriguing.

'It is nice,' Georgina agreed. 'But there's lots of work involved. At times we're like a jam factory here.'

Her smile faded for a moment. Then she added, 'But I'd rather be here, working hard in the sun, than in England, working hard in the rain.'

Sam smiled. 'You've been here a long time, haven't you? I think I remember Mum talking about it when you first came.'

'Quite a few years, yes.' Georgina did a rapid calculation. 'Coming up to twenty, actually. I'm a real expat.'

'I don't think I knew about Hugo. I can't recall Mum ever mentioning him.'

'No?' Georgina smiled. 'Well, I don't think she has ever met him. It's such a long time since she and I met even.'

'He seems very nice, and he's very handsome.'

Georgina nodded, 'Oh, he is. He's the apple of his mother's eye!'

Sam laughed. Privately, she was wondering why Mum had never mentioned him. Georgina might have been here all of twenty years, but Hugo was older than that, a lot older. He was more like her own age. So he must have been around when Georgina and her ex-husband came out here. It seemed odd that Mum had never said anything about him, and Sam was pretty sure she had not.

*   *   *

Georgina showed Sam to her room, and then left her to unpack and rest for a while. Sam was grateful. She was glad to have the chance to relax and recover from the journey. She had been on the move since very early that morning. It seemed even longer than that, as her last night at home had been pretty well sleepless. She had been so excited and apprehensive. A 7.00 am flight meant getting to the airport by 5.00, and a 3.30 wake-up call. It was something she

40

wouldn't care to do very often. No doubt Mum and Dad, who had taken her to the airport, wouldn't either, she thought with a rueful smile.

But she was here now, and it was so exciting to be here. Georgina was lovely, and this place ... She shivered with delight. Casa Largo. It was absolutely gorgeous. She couldn't believe how beautiful it was. She was so lucky to be here.

Her room, too, was wonderful. It was a big attic, with a sloping ceiling and a dormer type window from which she could, she fancied, just see the sea so many miles to the south. At least, there was a horizontal line in the hazy distance where it looked as though the sky finished and something very like sea started. How lovely, she thought happily. A sea view!

She grinned as a thought occurred: she would have to ask Georgina if you could see more of the sea when the tide came in!

She turned away from the window

41

and began to examine the furniture. It was old, and old-fashioned. A mixture of things, some possibly brought from Georgina's old home in Leeds and others that were obviously local and traditional. The two easy chairs, for example, could have come from somebody's granny's house, while the dressing table of dark wood was very much a piece of local artisan craftwork. What a mixture!

No matter. It looked perfect together. Just right for an old farmhouse like this. No-one choosing to stay here would want state-of-the-art, contemporary-styled furniture, and no-one would expect it. Nor did she.

Unpacking didn't take long. One other good thing, she thought, as she put her dresses away in the big wardrobe, was that there would never, ever be danger of damp here. Not a hint of it as she opened drawers and cupboards. This room, this house, had slumbered too long under radiant sunshine.

The room was not en suite but it did

have a delightful pairing of a porcelain wash basin and jug. She poured some water into the bowl and gently washed her face. Then she dabbed it dry with a towel taken from a nearby pile. Next she brushed her hair. Then she felt ready to face the world again — and for some lunch.

★ ★ ★

Halfway down the stairs she paused, hearing raised voices. It sounded like Georgina and a man in conversation. Something unfortunate or unpleasant seemed to have happened.

'I really need the money,' she heard the man say. 'Now! I mean it, Georgina.'

'Just go, Simon!' she heard Georgina respond with evident exasperation. 'Please. Just go. I'll see you tomorrow.'

Sam frowned and waited a long moment. When she heard a door slam she made her way down the remaining stairs.

'Problems?' she asked as she entered the kitchen, feeling a need to say something.

Georgina looked round and gave her a wan smile. 'Problems? No, not really. Just someone being difficult — as usual! Anyway,' she added, 'it's nothing for you to worry about.

'Come on! Sit down. Lunch is ready. Let's eat. Then we can discuss what I would like you to do while you're here in Casa Largo.'

Sam smiled and sat down at the table. She wondered if the seemingly difficult Simon was also part of the house's establishment.

'Simon?' Georgina repeated, when Sam asked who he was. 'Simon's a pain in the neck sometimes. That's what he is! But I do love him so.'

6

Georgina was right. There was plenty of work at Casa Largo. Much of it involved cleaning and laundering. Now the summer season had begun, guests were arriving and departing continually. Some came for a week or two, others for only a few days. And every time someone left, there was a cottage to clear. Bed linen to be changed and laundered. Fridges emptied and cleaned. Floors swept and washed. Forgotten property forwarded to departed guests. Georgina and Sam did most of it themselves, with the help at weekends of a girl from a nearby village.

Thankfully, so far as Sam was concerned, the cottages were self-catering. So there were no meals to be prepared. Nor was there any work to be done in the pristine garden. A local man Georgina employed part-time did all that very well indeed. He also looked after the pool.

Then there was Hugo, who appeared from time to time, but who never seemed to do anything very much. Perhaps he had a job elsewhere? She wasn't altogether sure if Hugo actually lived at Casa Largo either. That must be it, she thought. Perhaps he just came to see his mum.

And there was Simon, who seemed to come and go without ever doing very much either. Most of the time he was around he kept to the office, drinking endless cups of coffee.

Sam found it a little frustrating at times that neither of them helped with the cleaning. There was so much that needed doing. More of a helping hand from either or both of Georgina's two men would have been more than welcome. She really did wonder how on earth Georgina had managed before she had arrived on the scene. No wonder Mum had got the idea that she needed help, a lot of help.

The language thing was right, too. All the guests were from the UK, which was where the Casa Largo advertising was directed.

'It just makes things so much easier,' Georgina confided. 'I can't be doing with translating everything into German, French and what have you. Dutch, probably. We couldn't afford it!'

'It could be even worse, Georgina. There are twenty-eight member states in the European Union. In Brussels they have to translate every document into at least that many languages.'

Georgina visibly shuddered. 'Don't get me started on that subject!' she warned.

* * *

Sam decided that when she had found her feet she would tackle Georgina about Hugo and Simon, and see if they couldn't be persuaded to do more to help. Not yet, though. She was the new kid on the block. Besides, at the moment, it was just something too low in her list of priorities. Apart from anything else, she found the work exhausting, satisfying but very tiring.

That's what came, she supposed, of having spent so long working in an office. She just wasn't used to manual work. She had no stamina for it. Next time she spoke to Mum, she thought ruefully, she would apologise for not having helped her more when she was at home.

* * *

Then something happened to move the Hugo/Simon question a little higher in her list of priorities. It wasn't an edifying spectacle. Sam was in one of the cottages, putting the final touches to preparing it for their incoming guests, when she heard raised voices nearby.

'I asked you — told you — two days

ago to sort that television out!' she heard a man's voice say. 'And what have you done? Nothing, as usual. We have people coming in today. They'll want a TV. When they find it doesn't work, what will they say? Who will they blame? I know who I'll blame!'

The more Sam heard, she came to realise the voice belonged to Simon. The second voice, when it came, she didn't recognise. It wasn't until she looked through the window that she saw it belonged to Hugo.

'I've been busy,' she heard Hugo say. 'I can't do everything at once.'

'You've had two days!'

'I also had the website problem to sort out. Mum asked me to do that first. It took time.'

'Don't give me that! You're bone idle. That's your trouble. If I had my way . . .'

'Well, it's not up to you, is it?' Hugo said spiritedly. 'Who do you think you are, anyway?'

'Clear off!' Simon said wearily. 'Get

out of my sight. I'll find somebody else to do the job.'

'Gladly!'

Real anger and frustration there, on both sides, Sam thought sadly. It sounded as if they absolutely hated each other. How awful. The exchange just seemed to sour the whole atmosphere at Casa Largo. And what on earth would visitors think if they overheard more in the same vein?

But the exchanges at least indicated that the pair of them did do things around the guesthouse. It had been premature to conclude they did nothing at all.

★　★　★

'Do Hugo and Simon work for you?' she asked Georgina when she had the chance to bring up the subject. 'I mean, do they have regular jobs here?'

'Not all the time.' Georgina shrugged and added, 'They're part of the family. Yes, they do lots of things for me.'

'They were having a terrible argument this afternoon.'

Georgina sighed wearily. 'Again?' she said.

Sam nodded. 'It was just as well none of the guests were around to hear it.'

'I do wish they would leave each other alone,' Georgina said. 'I'll have to have a word with them both again.'

She didn't seem inclined to explain any further. So Sam left it there for the time being. It seemed a very odd situation. But, she reminded herself, it was nothing to do with her really. She was the newbie here. All the same, it did bother her, and it left her puzzled.

7

Much as she tried to put it out of her mind, it soon became apparent that angry exchanges between Hugo and Simon were not uncommon. Usually, it was Simon doing the shouting, apparently near the end of his tether with the unfortunate Hugo. He seemed to be forever finding fault with the younger man about something. But Hugo did his share of shouting, too.

It seemed very unfortunate, and much to be regretted. As to the rights and wrongs of it, she had no idea. Sometimes she just wanted to bang their heads together and tell them both to cut it out. She also wished Georgina would get hold of the situation properly, and sort it out somehow. After all, she was the centrepiece. The men revolved around her, partner, mother and owner of Casa Largo. No doubt, though, she acknowledged, that would be easier said than done.

* * *

There were others who appeared at Casa Largo from time to time who were no such mystery. Georgina had lived in the area for a long time, and she had made plenty of friends. In the main, they were expats like her, some of whom had lived in the Algarve even longer than she had. Not all were people Sam would have chosen as friends, but she was learning tact and patience to a degree that might have surprised her former colleagues in the office at MacDonald & Flanagan Ltd.

Denise and Graham, originally from Surrey, for example, were a wealthy and heavy drinking couple who bored her to tears when they didn't actually outrage her. Bleached blondes, both of them, from years in the sun doing nothing but partying and playing golf, they opened and drank bottle after bottle of wine the first time they came for dinner. Sam watched with awe.

'It's so wonderfully inexpensive,' Denise told her. 'Isn't it, darling?' she added, to draw Graham into a conversation Sam was already desperate to escape.

'It certainly is! You'll love it here,' Graham affirmed, as if the cost of wine was a principal consideration when it came to choosing where to live.

'Have you lived here long?' Sam asked cautiously.

'Forever!' Denise assured her cheerfully. 'And we've never looked back. You won't either, once you've got used to the easy pace of life here.'

Sam wondered about that. She really did. Her reason for being here was very different to theirs. She was here to work, and to sort her life out. They seemed to be here to party. Grudgingly, she did admit to herself that a lot of people would find nothing very wrong with that. It just didn't appeal to her.

Fortunately, Hugo appeared just

then, and Denise turned her attention to him. Hugo responded to her no doubt well-meant queries in monosyllables for a minute or two. Then he helped himself to a chunk of artisan bread and a plate of olives and just turned his back and walked away, leaving Denise stranded in mid-sentence. Sam struggled to hide a smile.

'That boy!' Graham muttered.

'He doesn't get any better, does he?' Denise said plaintively to Georgina.

Their host just laughed and diverted them with a query about their forthcoming trip to Lisbon. It seemed to be a shopping expedition in prospect. Sam lost interest. She felt a certain kinship with Hugo, who no doubt had suffered Denise and Graham's company many, many times.

Georgina, of course, was an absolute martyr, she decided. There wasn't a mean or impatient bone in her. There couldn't be if she continued giving Denise and her husband invitations.

'May I ask,' Sam heard then, 'if you have done any walking since you arrived in Casa Largo?'

She turned and smiled at the elderly gentleman sitting next to her at the table. Randolph, he was called. White-haired, avuncular, quiet, still sitting with his first glass of wine, he was someone to turn to with relief.

'None at all, I'm afraid,' she confessed. 'There simply hasn't been time. Also, it's so hot here, which is wonderful in one way but less so in others.'

Randolph chuckled. 'You'll soon get used to the heat. And you should make time, my dear. We are in beautiful hill country here, and at this time of year the wild flowers are quite spectacular. Go in the early morning. That's the best time. The air is so cool for the first few hours after the sun comes up.'

'Early morning?' Sam smiled. 'I'm not sure I could manage that. I need my sleep, especially after the way Georgina works me so hard!'

'Alter your daily timetable, and your body clock, if needs be. That way, you'll make the best of your time here.'

'Are you a walker?'

Randolph shook his head. 'Alas, no longer. I can't walk far these days, but I do what I can. And I still like the early mornings for the light.'

'Oh, yes. Georgina said you were an artist?'

'I like to paint, it's true. That's why I settled here many years ago. But mostly I am a failed artist. There, I admit it!' he added with a chuckle. 'Mostly I have taught painting, rather than produced it. Those that can, do, you know; and those that can't, teach. There is some truth in the old saying, even if it is not entirely fair.'

Sam smiled. 'Do you still teach?'

'I do. Not many students now, I'm afraid, but I still have a few.'

She had the impression he wasn't unhappy about that. Nor should he be. Teaching seemed an honourable way to spend one's time, especially at

Randolph's advanced age. Better, by far, than doing nothing but drink volumes of cheap wine, she thought, trying hard not to look across the table with disdain at Georgina's other guests.

'Have you been here a long time, Randolph?'

'Oh, yes.' He nodded indulgently to the far side of the table, where Denise and Graham were in full flow. 'A lot longer than some, I might add.

'My pension goes further here than back in England, you see. For some of us expats, as I suppose we must be called, that's an important consideration.'

'You're such a variety of people, you expats, and you all seem to live so differently,' Sam mused. 'Yet you meet each other often, and . . . ' She stopped, hand going to her mouth in apology. 'Oh, I'm sorry, Randolph! That came out wrong. I didn't mean to imply criticism of anybody.'

'And no offence taken,' Randolph

said with a twinkle. 'I know exactly what you mean, my dear. But in many ways it's a strange life for us here. We live in a local community, a very pleasant community I might add, but we can never really be part of it.

'Instead, we become part of the Algarve's expat English community, with its own newspaper and its own social functions — even its own bars and restaurants. Some of us don't even do that. There are those who simply live disappeared lives here, and are evidently very content to do so.'

Disappeared lives? Sam thought with a smile. How poetic, and yet sad, too. She could imagine that condition. 'Disappeared lives'. She must remember that phrase.

'What do the Portuguese people think about it all?'

'I've often wondered,' Randolph said with a wry smile. 'But perhaps Hugo is the best person to ask about that. He should know. All I can say is that, on the whole, the Portuguese people are wonderfully kindly and tolerant.'

He straightened up in his chair and added, 'And now I must leave you, I'm afraid. Otherwise, I shall miss the best of the light in the morning. I'm so very glad to have met you, my dear, and I do hope you enjoy your summer amongst us.'

'Thank you, Randolph. I hope we meet again.'

'I'm sure we will,' he assured her. 'You can be certain of that. The expat world is a small one, and inevitably you will find yourself part of it.'

'Not going already, Randolph?' Graham called.

'I am afraid so. I have work to do in the morning, and I like to get at it early.'

'Ah, work!' Graham replied, looking puzzled. 'What's that?'

Disappeared lives, Sam was still thinking. She felt she knew already what it meant.

8

For the first couple of weeks Sam didn't go far from Casa Largo, as she familiarised herself with the geography and the rhythms of the place. There was work to be done every day, but it didn't take all day. There was still plenty of time left over to wander through the garden and meander down the road to the nearby village, and along the way to stand and marvel at an old donkey-worked well that once had irrigated the field where it stood.

Now the field was abandoned, like a lot of others in the area, and the well was full of water. Despite appearances, the Algarve seemed to have plenty of water, but all of it was underground. Rivers and streams, fed by the winter rains, were nearly all seasonal, and quite dry by early summer. Sam let her imagination fill them with water again, and wondered if she would still be here when next the winter rains came. It seemed unlikely.

A couple of times she went into Sao Bras de Alportel with Georgina to buy provisions and postcards to send to parents and friends. Already, after such a short time, everyone she knew seemed so far away. She didn't want to be forgotten.

Then there were the evenings, when she and Georgina usually sat outside on the terrace, and sipped wine, and home-made lemonade and coffee, and talked. They were lovely times, watching the lemons swell on a nearby tree and listening to the gentle rustle of the palms in the soft evening breeze and to the buzz of the cicadas all around them.

'Do you miss England?' Sam asked one evening.

'Not really.' Georgina yawned. 'I don't think about it much any more. There's no-one left there for me now. No close family, and not many old friends that I'm still in touch with. I suppose I've always been a people person, not a place person. And most of my friends — and the people I know — are here now.'

Sam wondered if Mike, Georgina's ex-husband, was in that category. She had met him once, a long time ago, but now had only a vague memory of him. She wondered what had become of him, but didn't like to ask. No doubt that would only uncover old wounds. Besides, Georgina seemed to have a partner in Simon now. It was no time to be talking about an ex-husband, especially one she couldn't really remember.

'What happened with your boy-friend?' Georgina asked suddenly. 'Did you two just fall out?'

It seemed so unfair of her to ask, given that Sam had been mentally tiptoeing around Georgina's own situation, but Georgina wasn't to know that. Sam couldn't ignore the question, or decline to answer it, but she didn't want to talk about Steve. Already he was fast receding into the distant past, where unpleasant memories were kept.

'Oh, he just met someone else,' she said with a shrug.

'So that was that?'

She nodded and bit her lip. She didn't want to talk any more about it. So far as she was concerned, Steve was part of her past now — like her old job with MacDonald & Flanagan.

'A bit like what happened with me and Mike,' Georgina said. 'It's hard, isn't it?'

Sam just shrugged. She stared at a distant hill, and wondered what animals roamed over its rocky summit as night fell. Deer? Ibex? Possibly even lynx. She had read they were around, too.

'Well, we have a busy day ahead of us tomorrow,' Georgina said with a yawn, getting to her feet and ready to retreat indoors. 'Three lots moving out of the cottages, and three more coming in by evening. I've asked Esmeralda to come in especially to help us.'

'That's good.'

Esmeralda. The village girl. Sam liked her. She was pleasant and hard-working, and Sam knew already that preparing three cottages in one day would be hard going for herself and Georgina.

'The day after should be quiet, though?' she suggested.

'Thankfully.'

'I might go into Sao Bras, in that case. I'd quite like to have a bit of a wander on my own, if you don't mind?'

'Not at all. Take the car. You have a UK licence, I assume?'

'Oh, yes. I've had one for many years.'

'No, I mean with you. Take it, just in case you get stopped. The law requires you to. Take your passport, as well. You're supposed to have identification with you at all times in this country.'

'Really?'

'Really.'

It was another way in which Portugal was different to England. Sam wasn't sure she liked that. It seemed a bit draconian. But no doubt you got used to such things.

* * *

'Evening, ladies!'

'Oh hello, Simon!' Georgina said with a big smile. 'I was wondering where you'd got to.'

'Work, work, work — that's me!' He grinned and gave Georgina a peck on the cheek. 'How's things, Sam? Enjoying yourself? Exhausted?'

She smiled. 'Working hard, anyway. Yes, thanks. I am enjoying myself. It's lovely here.'

Simon nodded and turned back to Georgina. 'We need to talk,' he said.

'Again?' Georgina looked worried.

'Again.'

Sam stood up and excused herself. She was pleased to have the chance to escape. Those few words were the most Simon had spoken to her so far, and she wasn't eager to remain in his company. Simon was not her idea of someone with whom she wanted to spend time on a beautiful evening like this.

She did wonder, once again, though, exactly how Simon fitted into things. He and Georgina were obviously an item, but he didn't actually live at Casa Largo even though he appeared quite frequently. Then there were all the times she had heard him being unpleasant to poor Hugo. She hadn't forgotten either his demand for money from Georgina the very first day she had been here. What had that been about?

★　★　★

Back in her room, she took out her mobile and phoned home. It still surprised her that she could do that, but the truth was that her server seemed to work better here than it had done back in Northumberland.

'Hello, Dad! It's me. How's things?'

67

'Sam! We were just talking about you.'

'Why? What have I done now?'

He laughed and said, 'We were wondering how you were getting on. Warm enough for you?'

'Oh, yes. Too warm, if anything. And they say there's more heat to come, a lot more.'

'It would be good for my tomato plants,' he said wistfully. 'I think I'm going to have another poor year in the greenhouse.'

'I'll send you some tomatoes, Dad. Don't you worry about it! Is Mum there?'

Their conversation was nice and easy, a matter of keeping in touch with events and people. Nothing out of the ordinary had happened back in Fenham, Sam was relieved to hear. That gave her the opportunity to tell in detail what had been happening to her. There was so much new experience, so much to tell and share.

'Yes, Georgina's lovely,' she assured

Mum. 'She's really nice. I like her very much, and Casa Largo is gorgeous. Oranges and lemons on the trees in the garden, would you believe? It's wonderful.

'There is just one strange thing. There's this man around sometimes called Simon. I can't make my mind up about him, to tell you the truth. I don't like him very much, but Georgina seems fond of him. Has she ever mentioned him to you?'

'Simon? Oh, yes. He's her boyfriend, or partner, or whatever they call them these days. They've been together a while, I believe.'

'He doesn't seem to actually live here.'

'Well, I wouldn't know about that. I just know Georgina has mentioned him from time to time in her letters.'

'Oh, well. That explains that, then. At least I know who he is now.'

'He's not difficult, is he?'

'Not to me, no. But he can be unpleasant with other people.'

'Just keep out of his way, then.'

'You're right. That's the best thing to do. Oh, yes! There's something else I was going to mention. Did you know Georgina has a son, Hugo?'

There was a pause for thought before Mum said, 'Yes, I did know about him, but not much. He'll be about your age, I think.'

'Probably. But you've not met him?'

'No, I haven't. I suppose it's many years since Georgina and I last met. Mostly it's been just Christmas cards over the years.'

'I see,' Sam said doubtfully. 'I thought I'd not heard of him. Why didn't you ever mention him?'

'To be honest, I'd forgotten all about him. Georgina has never said much, and I've never seen him. There's something strange, something special, about him,' Mum added vaguely, 'but I can't remember what. Anyway, he'll be a nice boy, I assume?'

'Young man, actually Mum!'

'Oh, I suppose he is by now.'

'He seems pleasant enough, but a bit shy, not that I've seen much of him. I don't think he lives here now either.'

'Beware men who appear shy, dear! Your father was shy until after I'd married him. If I'd known then what I know now . . .'

'Stop it, Mum!' Sam laughed. 'I know he's listening. Stop teasing him.'

'I'd better, I suppose. He's looking upset now.'

★   ★   ★

Well, Sam thought afterwards, that conversation had explained one or two things. But it had also made her wonder about one or two more. So far as Simon was concerned, it was none of her business what Georgina saw in him, especially if they had been together a long time. What he did and where he lived was still a mystery, but all that was nothing to do with her.

And at least Mum knew of Hugo, even if she hadn't ever mentioned him.

Still, that was probably what happened when you didn't see old friends for years, decades even. How they lived now, and their children, could well be a mystery of which you knew next to nothing. You would just remember your friends as they used to be — single and child-free.

Just like me! she thought wryly. Was that how her friends back in Newcastle would remember her?

9

The nearby town, Sao Bras de Alportel
— or simply Sao Bras, more usually
— was small and quiet. It served the
surrounding agricultural area, and
Georgina said about 12,000 people
lived there. That meant it had all the
usual amenities, such as shops,
restaurants and banks. It had almost
everything, in fact, that a small
provincial town needed, including a
church that seemed far too big for a
place of its size. Once, during the
town's heyday as a centre for cork
production, it had even had a bishop.
That, Sam decided, probably explained
the huge church.

In an hour, she could have walked to
the centre of the town from Casa
Largo, but instead she opted to take up
Georgina's offer of the loan of her car.
It would give her some much-needed

experience of driving on the wrong side of the road and changing gear with her right hand, both of which were manoeuvres that were a bit daunting to contemplate.

She managed. She managed very well, actually. Parallel parking in the main street was a little difficult — everything was the wrong way round somehow — but the actual driving was OK. When she switched of the ignition she grinned, feeling quite proud of herself. Yes! she thought triumphantly. I can do this. I've done it!

So she could do something right. What would Steve have had to say about that? That he was astonished, probably, given that basically he had believed her to be inept. Over time, lack of confidence in a person can sap their self-confidence — and even help make the opinion come true. So sometimes she had used to wonder if Steve wasn't right.

Stop it! she told herself firmly. No more of that. Steve was her past, not her present. And still less her future. This was where she was now, for the time being at least. Forget about Steve, and might-have-beens. She was determined to make a success of what she was doing here.

What was it called again, this town? It was such a long and strange name, she could never remember it. She peered around until she saw the name on a shop front. That's it! she thought triumphantly with the joy of recognition: Sao Bras de Alportel. A funny-sounding name, poetic even, but the town was giving her a fresh start and even now she was ready to like the place.

It was a town with a long main street of twentieth-century buildings — shops, offices and little apartment blocks. Trees had been planted along the edge of the pavement in recent years, and their bright new green, set against the predominant building material of white concrete, promised much for the future.

Georgina had been right about it being quiet, though, Sam thought as she walked along the main street. Quiet and old-fashioned summed it up pretty well. The shops were all a bit dreary-looking, as well, unfortunately. Functional, but not much more than that.

The shoes and clothes in some of the shop windows were mostly hideous to her eye. The handful of non-essential shops, selling newspapers and toys, books and ornaments, were not very inviting either. Food and household essentials were sold from a couple of small, cluttered shops that billed themselves as supermarkets but would have been lost amongst the aisles of a Tesco or an Asda. But at least they existed, and they did seem to carry all the essentials.

Sam didn't think she would be buying much here, though, other than necessities. Still, she wasn't here for the shopping, was she? She stopped and looked around. Where were all the people? There were no crowds in sight, and not much traffic either, despite it being the town centre.

That made it all the easier for her to spot Hugo crossing the street a little way ahead of her. She smiled as he gave a little youthful skip, and she wondered what he was up to. Since her arrival at Casa Largo, she had only seen him a few times, and there had been little opportunity to do more than smile and wave a greeting from a distance. Mostly, she seemed to hear him being shouted at by Simon, and occasionally responding in a heated way himself. But he was nice-looking, and she did like what she had seen of him.

She still had no real idea of what Hugo did around Casa Largo, but whatever it was, it wasn't much. Georgina had not expanded on her initial explanation that 'he did things' around the place. In fact, she had said virtually nothing more about him at all. Odd, really.

Still, she really shouldn't be so disparaging about Hugo. He hadn't been unfriendly or rude to her. Mostly he had managed to avoid her. He had behaved as if she wasn't there, behaviour she attributed to shyness. She could understand that.

Anyway, she thought with a sudden grin, she had enjoyed the way he had shown his disdain for Georgina's appalling friends, Denise and Graham. That had enlivened what until then had promised to be a rather dull evening. That and Randolph, of course. She had enjoyed talking to him.

All the same, she did wonder how Hugo spent his days, and even what he did for a living. Surely it couldn't just be whatever it was he did around Casa Largo?

Oh well, she reminded herself yet again, it was nothing to do with her really. She didn't know how long she would be here, but she felt confident she could survive not knowing much more about Hugo. Or Simon, for that matter.

* * *

Moments later she discovered where at least some of the missing Sao Bras residents were. Just off the main street she saw a building throbbing with people, and with a lot more sitting outside at pavement cafés. She headed that way herself, thinking a coffee would be very welcome.

As she drew closer, she realised the building was a market hall. She passed through the entrance and found herself engulfed by the crowd pressing around the stalls selling local produce: fresh fish, and fruit and vegetables. Around the perimeter of the building there were also little butcher and bakery shops. Crowd chatter and the cries of the traders filled the air, making her ears ring.

Such a buzz! she thought with a happy smile. So this was where everyone was. She gazed with wonder at the bewildering variety and abundance of what was on offer. Enormous peppers and the longest runner beans she had ever seen. Big potatoes so fresh they were still dusted with damp earth. Huge oranges and gorgeously fresh lemons, better even than those she had seen in Georgina's garden.

And fish! She had never seen cod this size. Monsters. She hadn't known they grew so big. Sea bass, too, and sea bream. Tuna. And great boxes of oysters and baskets of every sort of shell fish she had ever heard of, as well as some she had never seen before and hadn't even known existed. Crabs, still moving. Lobsters waving claws and tentacles in the air. And what were these extraordinary creatures? Prawns?

'So what will it be for supper?' she heard a voice behind her ask.

She glanced over her shoulder, unsure if the question had been addressed to her.

'Hugo!'

'Good morning. Sam, isn't it?'

She gave a wan smile, knowing that he knew perfectly well what her name was.

'Are you shopping, Hugo, or sight-seeing, like me?'

He laughed. Another surprise. He wasn't someone she had thought capable of laughter. 'Definitely not sightseeing. I'm a local, remember, not a visitor.'

'Are you really? I wasn't sure about that.'

He just smiled.

'Well,' she said hurriedly, 'I think it's wonderful here. I've never seen so much fish in one place, and the fruit and vegetables are just gorgeous.'

Hugo nodded and pointed. 'That crab is trying to grab you!' he warned.

She gave a start and moved back hastily. 'No, he wasn't!' she complained, when she looked round.

'No, he wasn't,' Hugo admitted with a grin. 'Buy you a coffee?'

She hesitated, but only for a moment. 'That would be nice,' she said.

10

Hugo shepherded her into a café inside the market hall. It was a place where small groups of elderly men in flat caps sat at round-top tables, drinking beer from little bottles, playing dominoes and talking men-talk, while women recovered over tiny cups of strong coffee from the exertion of accumulating their purchases of fresh fish and potatoes, beans and green peppers. Young mothers took the weight off, looking exhausted, while their babies gurgled and slept in buggies alongside their tables. Slow-moving elderly men and women, handicapped often by arthritis, were courteously helped through the doorway.

Sam looked around with interest, not letting her gaze fasten on anyone indecently long. An ordinary people's café, she decided. Ordinary folk getting on with their daily lives. And what good lives they seemed to live here. Perhaps not as much money as people at home had, and nowhere near as much to choose from in the shops, but the food they were buying was all so fresh and wholesome-looking. Local produce, in the main. Such good value, too. A single euro seemed to buy a huge bag of fresh broad beans or a pile of little fish she couldn't name. Enough to feed a family, anyway.

'The coffee is good here,' Hugo assured her with an anxious smile, perhaps fearing some unease on her part. 'And the pastries, too.'

She smiled at him. 'I'm sure they are!'

'We can go somewhere else?'

She shook her head. 'This is just fine, Hugo. Perfect. I like it here. It's so busy and lively. All these people!'

'They come to see their friends, as well as to shop,' Hugo said with a shrug. 'The Saturday market particularly is a big social occasion, as well as where people do their shopping.'

Was it Saturday? Of course! She hadn't even thought of it. She had just grabbed today to do some sightseeing because it had promised to be a quiet day at Casa Largo.

'How often is there a market, Hugo?'

'Every day, except Monday. And Sunday, of course.'

He was still gazing at her as if she were giving him reason to be concerned. He wore that worried expression she had seen the very first day she had been here, when he had been looking for Georgina and hadn't been able to find her. It was quite touching. He really did seem such a gentle person.

'Saturday,' she repeated slowly. 'We're so busy that I'd lost track of the days of the week. But there's nothing for you to worry about. Really. I like it here. I wouldn't want to be anywhere else. So stop worrying!'

His face cleared, the anxiety replaced by a warm smile. 'Good,' he said simply.

They sat down on ancient bentwood chairs at the only vacant table in the little café.

'Do you like your coffee strong and black?' Hugo asked, as a waitress zoomed in on them.

'Not really. I prefer . . . '

'Then you must always ask for 'milky coffee'. Otherwise, you'll be given what most people here drink — espresso.'

'*Bom dia!*' said a waitress, arriving with a pad and pencil to take their order.

'*Bom dia!*' Hugo responded. 'Good morning!' he added for Sam's benefit.

He turned back to the waitress and spoke to her at a little length in seemingly perfect Portuguese, sounding just like a local.

'*Muito obrigado,*' the waitress said, turning away.

'That means 'thank you very much',' Hugo translated for her.

'I'm impressed with your language skills,' Sam said with a smile.

Hugo just shrugged and changed the subject. 'How are you liking Casa Largo?'

'It's lovely. I really like it. I'm even getting used to the heat!'

Hugo smiled. 'This is nothing. Wait until July and August.'

She grimaced. 'That's what Georgina said. Will I cope?'

'You'll do fine,' he assured her. 'You'll be almost used to it by then.'

She was surprised how ordinary, how normal, Hugo seemed now she was with him like this. Not at all shy-seeming. She hadn't thought him capable of such a light-hearted sort of conversation. This wasn't the person she saw from time to time around his mother's house.

'Do you live in town, Hugo?'

He nodded. 'Yes.'

Nothing else. Just that. He didn't like talking about himself, it seemed. He wasn't like most of the men she had ever met.

'How about you?' he added. 'Where are you from?'

'Newcastle. I've lived there all my life, and that's where both sides of my family are from.'

'Northern England,' he mused, as if consulting a mental atlas of the UK.

'Why aye, pet!' she assured him with a chuckle. 'Geordie Land.'

Hugo smiled uncertainly.

'That's Tyneside talk for you.'

He nodded and looked interested, as if she had imparted some gem of obscure knowledge.

'What about you?' she asked. 'Where are you from?'

'Me?'

'Yes, you!' she said with a smile.

'Here, I suppose.'

'Here?' Sam said. 'Portugal?'

'Algarve. Sao Bras.'

'Oh! I assumed you were British.'

'Perhaps I am.' He shrugged. 'It's hard to say.'

'*Por favor*,' said the waitress, as she reached between them with their coffees and a couple of pastries.

'*Obrigado*,' Sam said, earning a smile.

'Now I'm impressed,' Hugo said.

He smiled the big, generous smile she had seen once or twice since they had sat down. She laughed.

* * *

Strange, she thought again, while Hugo was away ordering more coffee. He seemed a totally different person. She wondered why he could be so remote, rude even, at Casa Largo, and yet so pleasant, charming even, here. It was a mystery.

And he was charming, she thought with a secret smile as she watched him standing talking at the counter. Handsome, too. Tall and slim, strong-looking, tanned, and with an absolute mop of dark curls. He must have looked just as handsome at Casa Largo, but somehow she had not realised it. That probably said something about how busy Georgina kept her!

'Here we are,' Hugo announced proudly, returning to their table with a couple of things that looked half-way between pastry and cake. 'They go well with coffee.'

'Hugo! What are you trying to do to me? I'll be fat as a house.'

'Sssh. Don't even think such a thing.'

Loud laughter and protests from a distant table diverted them for a moment. Men playing some card game had reached a resolution. There were scowls as well as faces lit with delight. Now a fierce discussion was breaking out, the losers not happy, the winners ecstatic.

'The prize must be a big one?' Sam suggested.

'Oh, yes! The winners have to pay for a round of beers. The trouble is they say they haven't won enough money yet to pay for a full round.'

Hugo watched and listened for a moment. Then he turned back to her with a grin. 'So now they will play again to see who should have a free drink, and who loses out.'

'It will take all morning!'

'All day even.' Hugo shrugged. 'Who

knows? That is how it is here.'

'Don't they work, have jobs to go to?'

'They are fishermen. So their work for the day was finished long before they came here, long before you and I got up this morning probably.'

'Oh? They fish at night?'

'Yes, they do. The fish are more active then, and come nearer the surface. Also, in the poorer light the fish can't see the net so easily. So the fishing is easier at night.'

'That's interesting.'

The snippet of inside information reminded her how little she knew of the lives of people here, others than expats, of course. The likes of Denise and Graham. Hugo and Simon were not the only local mysteries.

'How else do people earn a living in Sao Bras, Hugo?'

'Apart from in shops and restaurants?'

She nodded. 'I know so little about ordinary life here.'

He shrugged. 'Many people are small

farmers, growing the fruit and vegetables you saw in the market. As for the rest . . . I don't know. Mechanics and builders, and so on. People have normal jobs, I think.'

'And what about you? What do you do for a living, Hugo?'

That stopped him. He frowned and looked away.

'I'm sorry,' she said. 'I didn't mean to pry. I was just wondering . . . '

He shook his head and looked at his watch. 'I must go,' he announced. 'I have remembered an urgent appointment. You must excuse me.'

He pushed back his chair and got to his feet, startling her.

'It was nice meeting you,' he said stiffly. 'Goodbye.'

Then he was gone, leaving her to finish her coffee alone and make her own exit.

So that went well, she thought with a sigh, uncertain what she was most: astonished or annoyed.

11

Sam counted glasses, and then plates. Four of everything. They were all there. Cutlery to check next.

'By the way,' she said over her shoulder to Georgina. 'I didn't tell you I bumped into Hugo in Sao Bras yesterday.'

'Oh?'

'I was heading into the market hall when he appeared. He invited me to have a coffee with him.'

Georgina was busy putting clean sheets on the beds. She scarcely looked up.

'So I had coffee with him in a little café in the market. We were getting along famously, or so I thought, when I must have said the wrong thing. I asked him what he did for a living, and he just got up and bolted.'

'There,' Georgina said, looking round.

'I think that's everything, isn't it?'

Sam glanced round and nodded. 'All done, I think. Anyway, Hugo. I mean, you've told me he does things for you, but he doesn't work here full-time, does he? I just assumed he had a job doing something else.'

'Let's go,' Georgina said, heading for the door.

'It was really strange.'

'Hugo is Hugo,' Georgina said with a tone of finality. 'He's my son. Just let him be.'

Eyebrows raised, Sam shrugged and followed her through the door. Obviously she had said the wrong thing again. What was it about Hugo? Why the mystery?

★ ★ ★

This was the green time of year in the Algarve. Late April, and the hills were cloaked in wild flowers. All along the roadsides even, there was cistus, the rock rose, everywhere in a stunning

93

variety of colours. Yet to Sam's eye the soil was parched, the surface of the ground baked hard. Not a hint of the seasonal streams and rivers that Georgina assured her could be raging torrents in the winter months. Only the fresh green grass, the wild flowers and the bright new leaves on the trees said there had been any winter rain at all.

She stood next to a fenced compound and watched several dozen sheep finishing off a small pile of hay that had been dumped there for them. They were poor-looking, ragged little things, not half the size of the sheep to be seen at home. It wasn't surprising. They spent their days in a dirt enclosure without a hint of growing grass, waiting for the next load of hay to be brought to them. Then they stretched out in what shade they could find, and waited, chewing sticks if they could find any. It was depressing to see them.

Voices came to her from the nearby house. She looked up to see a small group of men heading for a pickup truck loaded with construction gear. A cement mixer and a couple of wheelbarrows. Lengths of timber and bags of cement. Scaffolding poles. The truck looked dangerously overloaded even to Sam's inexperienced eye.

Two of the men shouted and waved to someone else beyond the house, on a track that wound its way up a small hill. Sam's eyes followed the track and picked up the distant figure coming down the hill at speed in a small cloud of dust. As the figure grew closer, she realised it was Hugo.

The men shouted again, urging him to hurry. He laughed and started jogging towards them. When he reached the group there was much hilarity and back-slapping. Then they all climbed onto the pickup, two in the cab and Hugo and the others in the back, slotted between the cement mixer and the other equipment, hanging on to the sides.

The truck set off with a lurch and

Sam watched it gather speed as it headed down the gravel track towards the road. She could no longer see Hugo. Like the others, he was immersed in a huge cloud of dust that enveloped them and billowed out behind the truck. Smiling, and coughing, Sam wondered what that was all about. She also wondered what it would be like here in the dry season, when there would be nothing to lay the dust.

* * *

Georgina was disapproving when Sam, forgetting what had been said earlier, reported her sighting of Hugo with gusto.

'You should have seen them!' Sam chuckled, remembering. 'All hanging on to this battered old truck as it raced off in a cloud of dust. I was waiting for someone to fall off, but somehow they all stayed on until they reached the road. I don't know what happened after that. Where do you suppose they were going?'

'I've no idea,' Georgina snapped. 'I've told him to keep away from that lot,' she added angrily. 'They're a no-good bunch of layabouts! I expect they were going to the nearest bar.'

'No, I don't think so. It looked to me like they were going to do a day's work,' Sam said, surprised by Georgina's vehemence. 'There was a cement mixer, and I don't know what else, in the back. Does Hugo do that sort of work? Building, construction?'

'I have no idea,' Georgina said again.

'Well, they seemed to be having a lot of fun,' Sam said, disappointed by Georgina's response to her tale.

★　★　★

They got on with their work. One of the recently vacated cottages was particularly grubby. Floors, the bath and much else besides needed a good scrub. In the heat, it was demanding work. Sam soon

97

found herself sweating heavily — not just perspiring, she thought, amused. When they finished she was looking forward to a swim in the pool, as well as a shower and a cold drink.

Her thoughts strayed back to Hugo, and then to Georgina's reaction when she told her about him. It was such a pity. Georgina was being terribly grumpy about it. She'd been amused, but not Georgina. So far as Sam was concerned, though, it had been good to see Hugo so obviously enjoying himself with his friends, and perhaps work mates. They had all been having such fun.

Over lunch Georgina seemed distracted, her mind not really on sorting out what they had to do for the rest of the day. Sam tried a few times to offer light conversation but Georgina seemed uninterested. So she gave up and relaxed, content to watch small clouds scudding across the deep blue sky.

'About Hugo,' Georgina said eventually. 'Just so you know. He has his problems. He always has had. And at times, it's been very difficult for me to deal with them, especially with not having a husband to share the burden.

'He's a loner, basically; he lacks the normal social skills. At present he's living in town as an experiment. I thought it a bad idea, but he insisted on it. So I gave way, and let him do it. But I expect him to come back here any day. In fact, I insist on him calling in most days for me to see how he is.'

Sam was staggered. For a moment, she was unsure what, if anything, to say. The last thing she wanted was to make more difficulties for anybody. And that included herself. As a newcomer here, she really had little idea what went on between the people at Casa Largo.

'He's not that bad, surely?' she ventured eventually. 'He was very nice to me the other day at the market. For a while, anyway. Until I said something that must have upset him.'

'Exactly! My advice to you, my dear, is to keep well clear of him. Hugo is impossible at times, but if you avoid him you won't have any trouble.'

Georgina got up and disappeared to deal with something in the wash house. Sam sighed and shook her head. All this gloom and mystery about poor Hugo was deeply troubling. And perplexing. Was he really so difficult? What on earth had the man done to deserve such a poor character reference from his mother?

What Georgina had just said didn't seem to tie in very well with the man she had seen and talked to in the coffee shop. But, then, what did she know?

She got up, intending to return to her room now they had finished with the cottage where they had been working. As she crossed the cobbled yard, she went past the separate block where the laundry room was. Someone was in there but she didn't pay any attention until she was past and about to open the front door to the house. Then she heard Georgina in full cry.

'No, Simon! Absolutely not.'

'But I do need it. I have to have the money by the end of the week. You know what will happen otherwise.'

'It's not possible. I've told you.'

'I'm not staying, in that case. Get someone else.'

'Oh, Simon!'

The exchange was bad-tempered and deeply disturbing. Georgina was obviously upset, and Simon was angry once again. Sam grimaced and went inside, not wanting to hear any more. What on earth was going on? What was all that about?

Money, Simon had said — again. He wanted money. Did he mean Georgina was refusing to pay him something he was owed? Was that it? It had to be. For one of his odd jobs, perhaps. But why wouldn't Georgina pay him?

Or was he just demanding money anyway? A horrible thought crossed her mind. Could it be that Simon was simply not a very nice man? It was possible that something rather ugly was going on beneath the surface.

There was Hugo, as well, of course, and the problems Georgina said she had with him, problems that Sam couldn't see.

She shook her head and lay on the bed when she reached her room. Casa Largo wasn't the happy, tranquil place she had hoped, and at first had thought, it was. Poor Georgina. She really did seem to have a lot to worry about.

12

Having met Hugo and talked to him face to face, Sam was inclined to take his side in whatever feud he was engaged in with Simon. So far as she could see, Simon was the unpleasant one. Hugo might be a bit shy and introverted, even a little strange perhaps according to his mother, but he wasn't rude or offensive, and he didn't shout and rave at people the way she had heard Simon doing.

For Simon, money seemed to be a big issue. Twice she had overheard him going on about money to Georgina, demanding that she give it to him. Quite rightly, Georgina had resisted and held out, even though it had been difficult for her. Simon and money. Sam wondered again what exactly the problem was.

He might be Georgina's partner, but

insisting that she give him money was ridiculous, as well as offensive. He had no right to do that. It was disappointing, too, that Georgina had not stopped him in his tracks and put an end to his demands, once and for all. Surely she couldn't be so dependent on him that he could do and say whatever he liked to her? Was that what it was, a psychological dependency?

She didn't know Georgina well enough to be able to say. But perhaps Mum did. She would have to find a way of asking her when they next spoke on the phone. She and Georgina hadn't seen anything of each other for many years, of course, and people do change, but Mum still might be able to shed a little light.

Of course, there were other possibilities. Like what? Well . . . She didn't really know offhand, but there were bound to be some.

For now, though, she decided, she would just keep her eyes and ears open, and take more notice of Simon, and what he was doing. That was all she could do. Other people's relationships were not her business. It was just that she didn't like to think of Georgina and Hugo being bullied. If there was anything she could do to put a stop to it, she would gladly do it.

★ ★ ★

The mornings were very busy at Casa Largo, but in the afternoons the work usually tailed off. That was useful because it was in the afternoons that Simon usually appeared. He was rarely around in the mornings, when Sam wouldn't have had the time or opportunity to keep an eye on him.

He was often there in the evenings, as well, but that was when he and Georgina liked to spend time together. She tried to keep out of the way then. It rather irked her that Georgina seemed so fond of Simon, given how he behaved to her and Hugo, but there was no doubt that she did. Personally, she would have shown him the door.

As for what Simon did when he was around Casa Largo, it was a little difficult to say with any certainty. Most of his time was spent in the office, doing goodness knew what. Getting in Georgina's way, probably. Otherwise, it seemed to be this and that. Checking the waste bins, one day fixing a fence, ordering the gardener about, telling poor Hugo off. Sometimes it was as if it was his place, not Georgina's.

Not that it was all bad, Sam acknowledged reluctantly. There were always plenty of things for somebody to sort out, and if not Simon, then who? She and Georgina were run off their feet as it was. Hugo appeared from time to time, but he didn't do much. In fact, he didn't stay long if Simon was around, which was probably just as well.

Sam began to feel very frustrated by all this, and she didn't feel she could demand answers or solutions from Georgina. She was neither family nor permanent staff; she was simply summer help. She knew her place. How long she would be able to keep a still tongue in her head, though, was uncertain. Meantime, there was Simon to watch very carefully.

* * *

One afternoon Sam had borrowed Georgina's car again and was about to drive into Sao Bras to do a bit of shopping for essentials. She checked her purse, making sure she had her driving licence and passport, and was about to start the engine when she saw Simon hop into his old pickup truck and race off out of the gate. She waited a minute or two and then started the engine. This was too good an opportunity to waste.

She stayed well back in case he noticed he was being followed. The road was twisty and often Simon's truck was out of sight, but come a long straight stretch and there he was again.

She assumed he was going into Sao Bras, but it was just a guess. She really didn't know much at all about Simon, and she had no idea where he lived. Georgina had volunteered very little and Sam had picked up next to nothing from speaking to him.

With her, at least, Simon had always been reasonably polite, and sometimes even friendly, but it didn't fool her. She had heard how he sometimes spoke to Georgina and to Hugo. He wasn't a nice man, in her opinion. In fact, she was coming to think he was a nasty piece of work.

He did head into Sao Bras. She had been right about that. But then she lost him. The one-way system and the tangled streets meant he soon disappeared once he reached the centre. She cruised around for a few minutes, hoping to spot his truck, but it didn't happen. With a grimace, she abandoned the chase and pulled into the side of the main shopping street to consider what to do.

She could do her bit of shopping, as planned, but it would still be too soon to return to Casa Largo. Now she was here, with Georgina's car, it was too good an opportunity to waste. She felt like making the most of things, even though there wasn't an awful lot you could do in Sao Bras. Still, she ought to be able to find something. She needed some time away from Casa Largo. She needed a change.

She parked, got out and did her shopping. Then she went looking for a nice little café where she might have a coffee or a glass of wine. Big day out! She smiled ruefully at the thought. So far, she had not had many of them. She had been too busy, and then too tired at the end of the day anyway.

Suddenly she saw a familiar face coming towards her. It was Randolph, the elderly artist she had met at Casa Largo on her first evening there. He was looking very dapper as he tapped his way along the pavement with his walking cane. Dressed in what she thought was probably a painter's smock, with a silk scarf draped casually around his neck, he looked every inch an artist — and he didn't care who knew it!

'*Boa tarde, Randolph!*' Good afternoon.

She delighted in using one of the small number of Portugese phrases she had acquired.

The old man stopped, peered hard and then smiled. 'My dear! *Boa tarde* indeed. How are you today?'

'I'm fine, thank you. And you?'

'As well as can be expected at my age,' he said with a cheerful grin. 'Has Georgina given you the day off?'

'We finished early, so I decided to come into town for a look round.'

'There's not an awful lot to see in our little town. Have you not seen it all already?'

She laughed and said, 'I shall never tire of it, the market particularly. I could come here every day to see that. Unfortunately, it's in the morning, isn't it? So I've missed it today.'

Randolph nodded and said, 'I agree with you about the market. It is the very heart of the town. I used to enjoy painting there very much.'

'I'm surprised you didn't get knocked over! All those crowds?'

'Oh, well. You know. People here are very courteous and considerate.'

She smiled. She could imagine people being careful to skirt carefully around him at his easel. He must have been a rare and interesting sight.

'I was just thinking of having a coffee somewhere, Randolph. Would you care to join me?'

'What an excellent idea! If you don't have anywhere in particular in mind, perhaps I can recommend a little place just around the corner from here?

'By the way,' he added, 'allow me to congratulate you on your excellent Portuguese language skills. You have made great progress already.'

'It's a start,' she said, laughing. 'I won't pretend I know much more.'

* * *

Randolph was pleasant company and, even better, he was not from Casa Largo. She was ready to talk to someone from outside, more than ready. Also, she thought, Randolph seemed like a bit of a gossip, and he might well be able to answer some of her many questions. He must know far more about the set-up at the house than she did. So bumping into him like this gave her a chance she was happy to grab.

He led her to yet another small café she hadn't known about, but one where he seemed to be well known. Having seen that she was seated at a table of which he approved, he spent a few minutes receiving and delivering greetings from the staff and several customers. Sam smiled indulgently. Charmingly, Randolph seemed to be a part of the community. She liked that.

He was very particular about his coffee, she discovered. Eventually he got some to his satisfaction and settled down to talk. He was good at that, too. Randolph was an amusing, entertaining conversationalist. No wonder he was so welcome at Casa Largo, she thought, and doubtless countless other places as well.

'You seem to know absolutely everybody here, Randolph.'

He chuckled. 'I've been here a long time, my dear.'

'What about the expats? Do you know all of them, too?'

'Most of them, I suppose, and a lot more who are no longer with us for one reason or another. I really have been here an awful long time, too long probably.'

She thought for a moment, wondering how to broach the subject on her mind, and then simply asked, 'Do you know Simon, Georgina's boyfriend? I saw him on the way here, and I was wondering if he lives in town.'

'Simon Kendrew? Yes. I believe he does live here. Don't ask me where, though. I don't get around as much as I used to do.'

'But you do know him?' she persisted.

'Not really, no. Not well, at least. He's a bit of a mystery, is Simon. He came on the scene several years ago, but I don't know where from or what he does here. I believe he helps Georgina out, but I don't know what else he does.'

Sam thought about it and decided to force the pace while she had the opportunity.

'I don't think he helps Georgina much. In fact, he seems to cause more trouble than help. He really is a very rude man at times. Not to me, though, I must say. I wouldn't let him be. But he is to Georgina, and also to poor Hugo. I have to admit I've been wondering about him, and why they allow him to get away with it.'

'He helps Georgina with the business side of things, as I understand it,' Randolph said vaguely.

'Oh? Ordering people about, and mending the occasional fence, is all I've seen him doing.'

Randolph chuckled. 'I'm sure Georgina told me that once. Of course, it must be all hands on deck at Casa Largo. I don't believe the financial situation is what Georgina would like. I'm surprised you haven't been required to mend fences!'

She smiled. 'Really, Randolph? Do you think there are financial problems?'

'Hanging on by a thread is perhaps the appropriate metaphor. Poor Georgina. She has worked so hard.'

'But why? The bookings seem to be good, and it's a lovely place.'

Randolph shook his head. 'Business is a mystery to me, my dear. I have no head for it. Nor, perhaps, does dear Georgina, when it comes down to it.'

Sam wondered if he was right about all that, and about Simon too. In what way could he be helping Georgina in a business sense? She couldn't imagine.

'Simon is not unlike a few people

who end up here,' Randolph added. 'Some of us have a very good reason, and come with a clear sense of purpose, but there are others for whom it is an escape. They have left their old life behind, and have no wish either to revisit it or to be reminded of it.

'Some, I fear,' Randolph added with a twinkle in his eye, 'have much to escape from, even the eye of the law in some cases. It is comparatively easy here to live a different life, and even to be someone else.'

'What do you mean? Assume a false identity?'

'That has been known. But I meant it in a more general sense. If no-one here knows you, you can re-invent yourself. It is entirely possible.'

That was undeniably true, Sam thought. It had long been known that Spain, and the 'Costa del Crime', which was not too far away, harboured many British criminals. Why not here, too?

Why not Simon even? That would fit

very well with what she knew of him.

She shook her head impatiently. 'What about Hugo, Randolph? How well do you know him?'

'Ah! Dear Hugo. Now that's a different story.'

Randolph glanced at his watch, pursed his lips and added, 'But I'm afraid to say that I really must be going now.'

Sam was disappointed. 'No time for another coffee?'

Randolph shook his head. 'Not here, at least, but you are most welcome to come home with me, and have coffee there.'

He looked at her expectantly.

'I would like that,' Sam said quickly. 'Thank you, Randolph.'

'In that case, I will have more time to tell you about Hugo.'

13

Randolph lived in a second floor flat in a quiet road running parallel to the main shopping street. It was an old, and old-fashioned, sort of place, with lots of rooms, more a mansion apartment than a flat. Every room was cluttered with books and bric-a-brac, paintings and pieces of gnarled wood that had been collected because in some way they appealed to an aesthetic eye. There was no doubting it. This was the home of an artist.

'What a lovely place!' Sam exclaimed. Turning to the window and wooded hills beyond, she added, 'You have a very pleasant outlook too.'

'Oh, I've been here so long I no longer notice the view,' Randolph said with a wry chuckle. 'It's the convenience of being in the centre of town that I appreciate most at my time of life. I used to like hills, but not any more. Life on the flat suits me perfectly these days.'

'So you don't get to Casa Largo very often?'

'Not as often as I used to, no. In fact, I only go nowadays when Georgina takes me. An invitation is not enough. Physically getting there is a lot more difficult than it used to be. I can't walk far, and I gave my car up a number of years ago. I had become a danger to the general population.'

Sam doubted that. She doubted that very much. But she smiled agreeably, and let Randolph pour her a glass of local wine to go with the coffee he was making.

'Tell me about Hugo,' she said when Randolph settled down at last. 'I'm ever so curious, and Georgina has told me nothing about him. In fact, she's more or less warned me not to even mention him. I have no idea why, and it intrigues me.'

'Ah, yes,' Randolph said, nodding. 'Poor Hugo.'

'Poor? Why poor? He's lovely! I met him in the market recently. We had coffee together, and he was very pleasant. At Casa Largo I catch only distant glimpses of him as he disappears. He smiles but he rarely speaks.'

'He's a sweet boy, Hugo, but rather a sad case. Devoted to Georgina, of course.'

'Scarcely a boy, Randolph. He's all grown up now. He must be about my age.'

'Yes, I suppose he is. But I still think of him as Georgina's ward. That's what he'll always be to me.'

'Georgina's ward? Whatever do you mean, Randolph?'

Randolph gazed at her with evident surprise. 'You don't know the background?'

She shook her head. 'No-one has told me anything about Hugo. Whenever I ask Georgina about something to do with him, she changes the subject or warns me off.

'All in all, I'm in a strange position at Casa Largo. There are these people around — Hugo and Simon, I mean — who I know nothing about. It's very frustrating. Besides, in a practical sense I need to know who they are and what they are responsible for. What's wrong with that? What's the mystery?

Randolph shook his head, as if to say he didn't understand it either.

'Anyway, why did you refer to Hugo as Georgina's ward? He's her son, isn't he?'

'Yes, of course he is. He is now, at least. But he wasn't originally. Georgina adopted him.'

'Oh?' Sam leant forward, very surprised. 'I had no idea, Randolph. I just thought . . . Oh, never mind what I thought! How did that come about?'

'Hugo was about two years old, I believe, when his parents were both killed in a terrible car crash here in the Algarve.

'The parents were both British, and they were very good friends of Georgina and her then husband, Mike. There were no close relatives for the boy, either here or back in the UK. So Georgina and Mike, who were looking after Hugo at the time, applied to keep him and bring him up. The court accepted their application, and for a time Hugo became their legal ward. Later, they adopted him, and he became their son.'

'I see,' Sam said thoughtfully. 'Poor Hugo indeed. But how wonderful that Georgina and Mike stepped in.'

'Yes.' Randolph nodded, and almost agreed. 'It was good of them, and good for Hugo. At least, it was the best thing that could have happened at that point. Far better than him being consigned to an orphanage, which would have been the alternative.'

'But?' Sam said cautiously. 'There is a but?'

Randolph waved a hand dismissing the concern. 'Not really. It's just that the poor boy finds himself stuck now, neither British nor Portuguese. Not really. I don't believe he has ever sorted that out. Should he be here, or there? With Mike long gone, Georgina is his only point of reference, just as he is for her, I suppose.'

Sam thought about it. A lot of things seemed more understandable now.

'Does he have . . . well, problems, psychological problems?'

'Hugo?' Randolph laughed at the idea. 'Of course not. He's a fine young man. Whatever gave you that idea?'

'Well, Georgina. She told me he was very introverted and vulnerable.'

'No, no! I won't have that at all. I'm afraid that's Georgina for you. I don't believe she has ever wanted Hugo to grow up, but he has. Oh, yes, he has!'

'Yet he doesn't live at Casa Largo. Did he ever?'

'Of course. All his life nearly. It's where he grew up. Not now, though. I believe he has a place of his own in town somewhere now. There's a story behind that, too.

'Basically, Georgina wouldn't hear of him leaving and getting a place of his own, but Hugo insisted on it. They had terrible rows over it, but Hugo had his way in the end. He probably said he would leave the area altogether if Georgina didn't stop objecting.'

'Well, she seems to have come round,' Sam said thoughtfully. 'Actually, she told me that it's an experiment, to see if he can manage on his own.'

Randolph chuckled. 'I'm sure that is how Georgina will see it. It will be how she reconciled herself to Hugo moving out.'

'Probably,' Sam said with a rueful smile. 'We all do that at times, don't we? Make allowances, and construct little stories to make the world fit better.'

Randolph nodded. 'All of us,' he agreed, looking at her with surprise, as if he hadn't expected such an insight from her.

* * *

Sam didn't learn much more from Randolph, but she left his apartment well satisfied. She knew far more now about both Simon and Hugo, and all sorts of pieces fitted together a lot better than they had done.

Randolph had certainly given her an understanding of Hugo's position at Casa Largo, and his occasional presence there. It was his home. Of course it was. He might have his own place now, in Sao Bras, but Casa Largo was where he had grown up and knew best. And Georgina was his mum, the only one he had ever known.

It was enough. She didn't need any more explanation. Thank you, Randolph, she breathed as she walked back to the car. I understand things now.

She also understood a lot more about Simon. Not everything, but enough to reinforce her opinion that he was trouble. In her opinion, Georgina had made a big mistake in ever getting involved with him. She suspected he had a lot to hide, perhaps even his true identity. The demands for money fitted in very well with the idea of a life on the run — from something. Could it even be that he was some sort of criminal? She was beginning to believe that it very well could. He was not a nice man at all.

Sam was more determined than ever that, for Georgina's sake and for Hugo's, she would do what she could to uncover Simon's secrets. She was not prepared to allow the man to continue bullying Hugo and deceiving and manipulating Georgina. Enough was enough. She had decided.

14

For a day or two Simon spent a lot of time at Casa Largo, and it was easier for Sam to keep an eye on him and watch what he did. He did do a few useful jobs in that time. So perhaps he wasn't a total waste of space, she decided. One of them was fixing a fence to stop marauding sheep from an adjacent field getting into the garden and eating their fill until someone noticed and chased them out again. She saw him collecting clean linen from the laundry, too, and even initiated a conversation with him there.

'It's good to get some help in here, Simon,' she said cheerfully. 'Georgina and I are struggling at times.'

'I can see that,' he admitted. 'I'm glad to help when I can. If I had more time, there would be a few other things I could do as well.'

'Oh, you have other work, do you?' she asked innocently.

He gave her a smile. Then he dropped the laundry basket and headed for the office, where Georgina was busy with some paperwork.

Oh, dear! Sam thought, amused. I must have said the wrong thing again. I'm good at that.

She waited to see if another disagreement between Georgina and Simon erupted. Thankfully, it didn't this time. Instead, they pored over some papers spread on a table. Sam waited a minute or two, and then gave up and headed for the next cottage. New guests were expected later that day.

She would dearly like to know what else Simon got up to when he wasn't here. Something no good, she suspected. Even criminal? Quite possibly. She wouldn't rule anything out.

★ ★ ★

Her suspicions were increased later that day, when during a coffee break she read an article in a local newspaper about illegal immigrants and foreign criminals who had taken up residence in the Algarve. Some of the resorts at the coast were awash with both, apparently, and false identities were readily obtainable by those with money, i.e. the foreign criminals. She didn't suppose the poor immigrants from Africa would have the money to legitimise their presence.

She frowned and wondered again if Simon might be one of those people Randolph had mentioned, people who had come here to leave their old life behind, and who had perhaps changed identities in the process. It was something worth thinking about. But how could she find out? Only by keeping her eyes and ears open. Realistically, that was all she could do at present.

'Hello, dear!' called one of the new guests. 'Working hard?'

'Oh hello, Mrs Stevens!' Sam straightened up. 'Everything all right?'

'Just fine, thank you. It's lovely here, isn't it?'

'Well, I think so,' Sam said with a smile.

'I don't know how you manage in the heat, though.'

'Oh, this is nothing,' Sam said airily. 'Wait till mid-summer!'

Just then, another guest, a Mr Mason, came hurrying towards her, looking quite agitated. Sam moved to meet him.

'Samantha! We've got a problem. Can you spare me a minute?'

'Of course. What is it?'

'There are ants in our cottage — thousands, millions, of them! My wife is terrified. She's locked herself in the bathroom.'

'Oh, dear! You must have left food out.'

'Food for the ants? Don't be ridiculous!'

'No, no! I didn't mean that. Come

on. Let's see what's happening.'

Georgina had told her that you couldn't leave food out. Everything had to be kept in the fridge or sealed containers. Otherwise a marauding column would come for it. But she hadn't seen the ants in action for herself.

She did now.

'Goodness!' she exclaimed with horror when they entered the Masons' cottage.

There were swarms of them. They were on the table and on the floor. They were all over some packaging on the kitchen table. Her heart beat faster at the sight, and she stood still in shock for a moment.

'What's that on the table?' she asked with a grimace, trying to keep an even tone.

'It's our lunch! My wife bought some barbecued chicken, ready cooked. It was warm. So we couldn't put it in the fridge.'

It had been left on the table. And now the dreaded ants had found it.

They were busy tearing it apart and transporting it, piece by piece, to wherever it was they lived. It was a fascinating spectacle, but not one for the faint-hearted, holiday makers or not.

Sam tried to pull herself together and avoid panicking. 'The first thing to do,' she said, determined to appear practical, 'is get rid of what's left of the chicken. You've lost your lunch, I'm afraid.'

She pulled out a rubbish bag, steeled herself and grabbed the mess on the table and thrust it into the bag. 'I'll be back in a moment,' she assured a worried Mr Mason, as she hurried off to the bins.

When she'd dumped the remains of the chicken, along with the ants refusing to let go, she called Georgina out from the office and told her what had happened.

'Oh, no!' Georgina groaned. 'I did tell them not to leave any food out.'

She disappeared back into the office

for a moment and reappeared with an aerosol can of what she said was ant killer. Then she went on the attack, with Sam guarding her back and trying to be calm about the situation in front of Mr Mason.

With the chicken gone, the numbers of ants were already much reduced, and Georgina made short work of those that were left. Like Sam, Mr Mason watched, fascinated now.

'That should do it,' Georgina finally pronounced. 'They shouldn't be back. Just don't leave any food out again, Mr Mason. Please.'

'No,' Mr Mason said shakily. 'We'll not do that again, don't you worry! Where on earth do they live, these things?'

'Who knows?' Georgina said. 'Ants are everywhere in warm places — in the ground and in buildings. This colony could have been here for centuries. But they are harmless — I must emphasise that — and they don't bother us normally. They just scavenge for what

133

they need. So we live with them. We have to.'

'They don't have them in Blackpool,' said Mrs Mason, putting in an appearance now the cottage had been rendered safe.

'No,' Georgina said, 'I don't suppose they do.'

Mrs Mason added, 'But I didn't want to go there. The weather isn't reliable.'

For a moment there was silence, everyone stunned by the inane comment. Then Sam laughed, and soon they were all at it, even Mrs Mason, the tension quite gone now.

*　*　*

On their way back to the office, Georgina said, 'I normally call out Simon to deal with an ant attack, but he's not here today.'

'He's good at that, is he?' Sam said innocently. 'Killing ants?'

'Oh, he is. He's a lot tougher than me.'

Why aren't I surprised? Sam thought.

'I'm glad my room is upstairs,' she added.

'Oh, they can get up there just as easily,' Georgina assured her with a chuckle. 'They just have to know there's something worth going for. Then they'll be there.

'You did very well, by the way, Sam. Thank you for not panicking and frightening the guests. When you've not seen them before, it can come as a bit of a shock.'

'Oh, I was shocked enough when I first saw them, but then I came to see that they were quite interesting. Fascinating, really. I mean, all they're doing is collecting food for their families, isn't it?'

'That's the Casa Largo spirit!' Georgina said, laughing with approval.

15

Quite by chance, Sam bumped into Hugo in town again, and once more they had coffee together.

'I'm beginning to think this is how you spend your time, Hugo — in coffee shops and cafés. Meanwhile, your poor old mum and I work like slaves at Casa Largo.'

'Somebody must,' he suggested with a grin.

'But why does it always have to be me? That's what it was like the last place I worked, before I got made redundant. If something wants doing, ask Sam. She's good at doing things, especially things no-one else wants to do, because they're tired or it's too hot, or something.'

'You got made redundant, did you? Is that why you're here?'

'I suppose it is, really. At least, that was the start.'

She pulled a face and added, 'I'd been there a long time, as well. But I wasn't the only one. Everyone lost their job. After a hundred-and-however-many years, the whole place went down the tubes. The firm went bust, and the receivers decided there was nothing to save. So it was a crash landing, with a lot of casualties. At least I didn't have a mortgage to pay or a family to support.'

'What did the firm do?'

'Made carpets, and such. Soft furnishings.'

'Sounds interesting.'

'Well . . . Perhaps it was, but no more than anywhere else, really. Not to me, at least. Accounts are accounts, wherever you happen to be. But I did like the place, and I liked my colleagues as well.'

'There must have been a lot of design work?'

Sam yawned. 'Sorry!' she hastened to say. 'I must have got up too soon this morning.

'You were saying? Oh, yes. Design.

Well, I didn't see anything of that side of the business. I just worked in accounts, as I said, and that was the same as accounts anywhere else. Why?' she added belatedly. 'Does design interest you?'

Hugo shrugged. 'It does, actually, probably with growing up here. Design, pattern — that sort of thing. The influence of the Moors is still here, you know. You must have seen the tile work, the ceramics, everywhere — all the floors and walls?'

'Not really. I haven't been anywhere very much yet. Too busy. But there's some at Casa Largo, isn't there? I've seen that, of course.'

He nodded. 'Mum has a few rugs in traditional patterns, too.'

She supposed she had noticed them too, vaguely, but without great interest. There were other things she was much more interested in, and there was far too much work to do.

Thinking of the old farmhouse, and what went on there, she said, 'You and

Simon don't get on too well, do you? You seem to do a lot of arguing.'

'That's true,' Hugo admitted. 'He tells me off all the time for not doing as much as he thinks I should, and then sometimes I shout back at him. Maybe it's a constructive relationship? I don't know really.'

'It doesn't sound like one to me. He seems to be a very difficult man.'

'In some ways, he is. But at heart he's a pretty good guy, really. He and Mum seem to get on well together.'

'But they have arguments, as well! I hear them. I think Simon must be difficult with everyone.'

Hugo shrugged. 'Maybe. I don't know.'

'Have Simon and your mum been together for very long?'

'A couple of years. I'm not really sure.'

He seemed eager to drop the subject of Simon, but Sam was not quite ready to give up yet.

'What does Simon do when he's not

at Casa Largo, which is most of the time? Does he have a job?'

'A business. He has a business. But don't ask me what it is. I'm not really interested.'

'And he has a house or a flat in town somewhere?' Sam persisted, still not ready to give up yet.

Hugo nodded.

She could see he had lost interest in the conversation — in her questions about Simon, at least — and she thought she had better change the subject or risk him storming off again.

She leant back in her chair, looked around at the throbbing little café and confided, 'You know, I'm getting to really like this little town.'

'Are you?' He smiled. 'Good. I'm pleased.'

'Why's that?'

Smiling, he said quietly, 'If you like it, you might stay a while.'

'Oh, Hugo!' She smiled back with surprise. 'You do say the loveliest things.'

'But I haven't told you why yet,' he protested.

'Go on, then. Disillusion me.'

But whatever Hugo had in mind didn't get said. Two young women marched into the café and made a direct line for him, laughing and crying greetings to everyone in the place.

One of them, a pretty little blonde with a lovely caramel complexion, wrapped her arms around Hugo from behind and cried, 'Here you are, darling! Suzy and I have been looking everywhere for you, haven't we, Suze?'

'Everywhere,' the other girl agreed.

Hugo seemed torn between delight and embarrassment once the initial shock wore off. He smiled awkwardly and shrugged at Sam. *What can I do?*

'Hello, Abby!' he said, chuckling. 'Where have you come from?'

Abby wrapped her arms even more tightly around him and said, 'We've been shopping in Faro, me and Suze. We've just got back.

'And what do we find?' she added, grinning at Sam. 'We find you've been two-timing us already!'

'Shame on you!' Suze added cheerfully.

'Me?' Hugo said, indignant. 'Never!'

'Sit down!' Sam urged with a smile. 'Please. I'm going soon anyway.'

They were a bright and cheerful pair. Both British, she decided. Very friendly. And pretty. With expat tans.

But what would Georgina say? Sam couldn't help wondering. It might not have ever occurred to her that Hugo was capable of attracting women. But he obviously was, and had. Here was the evidence.

'I'm Abby,' said the blonde girl as she pulled up a chair and sat down. 'And this is Suzy. We've not seen you before. Are you on holiday?'

'Hello! I'm Sam. No, definitely not on holiday. Anything but, in fact.'

Hugo belatedly came to her rescue at that point. 'Sam works at Casa Largo for my mum.'

'Oh, really? So how long have you been here?'

'Not long. I'm here for the summer. At least, I think I am.'

'Well, you've come at exactly the right time. Tell her, Suze.'

'Big party tomorrow night,' the other girl said. 'At my dad's place. It's my birthday. You're very welcome to come. Hugo can bring you, can't you, Hugo?'

'Probably,' Hugo said, glancing anxiously at Abby. 'Is that all right with you?'

'Oh, don't mind me,' Abby said airily. 'I'll get a taxi or something — or drive myself.'

'You won't drive yourself,' Hugo said firmly. 'We've been through that more than once. You'll lose your licence if you're not careful.'

'Phooey!' Abby looked at Sam. 'What do you say? Will you come?'

'Well . . . Thank you all very much,' Sam said uncertainly. 'But I'm not sure. I'll have to see how the work goes.'

'Phooey to that, too!' Abby scoffed.

'Just tell Georgina you're going party-ing. And that's all there is to it.'

*   *   *

It wasn't, of course. Not by a long way. There was a lot to think about. That evening, having got used to the idea that Hugo seemed to be quite the lad about town, whatever his mother thought, Sam wondered if she really wanted to get involved with the young, expat party crowd. She didn't want to end up like a clone of Denise. She hadn't come here to go down that route.

Then there was the fact that her availability really did depend on how things were at Casa Largo with Georgina. One or other of them ought to be there at all times, in case something went wrong or needed doing. It wouldn't be right for their guests otherwise. Possibly not even legal.

On the other hand . . . Well, Abby

and Suzy were a bit young for her, but she wasn't quite an old maid yet. And it would be a night out, and a chance to meet people.

In the event, Georgina said fine, go. So she went.

16

Hugo picked her up and they travelled in his car to a hotel she hadn't even known existed just outside the town. There were splendid views from a wide terrace out across Sao Bras and the hills beyond, and possibly the sea beyond them.

'Glad you came?' Hugo asked, seeing her fascination with the view.

'Oh, yes! Thank you for bringing me. But hadn't you better look for Abby now?'

'You're right. I should.' He looked a bit worried. 'Oh, here's the star of the evening!' he added, as Suzy approached at speed in a very slinky party dress.

'Sam! I'm so pleased you could come. Hi, Hugo!'

Sam smiled and congratulated the girl on her birthday, and also on her gorgeous dress. 'You look absolutely lovely, Suzy!'

'Why thank you, Sam! It's very kind of you to say so.'

Sam suspected she was well used to making a glamorous appearance. She really was a beautiful girl. But she was also modest and polite, and altogether a charming hostess.

Now she introduced Sam to a small group of friends nearby, and encouraged Hugo to take himself off to find Abby. 'Your name will be mud if you leave it much longer!' she called after him, laughing.

Hugo pretended to be frightfully concerned, causing more laughter. Sam smiled, too. She could see that these people all knew each other well. As Randolph had told her, the expat world was a small one.

'She's probably drunk by now!' Suzy added, urging Hugo to hurry.

'Already?'

'She's been here hours. We both have.'

'We all have!' said a man called Gerry, standing nearby.

'Hello, love!' he added in a Yorkshire accent, turning to Sam. 'Who are you? A tourist?'

'Not a tourist, no. A worker having a night off! I'm Sam. I work for Hugo's mum.'

'At Casa Largo?'

'That's right.'

'It's a grand place, isn't it? And Georgina's smashing. I don't know about her other half, mind, that Simon. Darling!' he called to a woman nearby. 'Come and meet Sam. She works for Georgina.'

'And that dreadful Simon?' the woman, Gerry's wife, said as she came over.

Sam smiled politely. 'Simon's there sometimes, but it's Georgina I came to help. She's an old friend of my mum's.'

'Oh?'

Simon didn't seem to be popular here, which didn't bother Sam very much. In fact, hardly at all. She happily began to talk to Gerry and his wife, Rhoda, who said they were retirees from Rotherham.

'Used to work for the Coal Board,' Gerry confided, 'before that woman sent the whole industry down the tubes.'

'Gerry!' his wife warned. 'This is a party, a birthday party for heaven's sake.'

Gerry rolled his eyes and stopped. For a dreadful moment, Sam had thought she was going to hear all over again about that dreadful Mrs Thatcher, who had been Prime Minister when Sam was at school. She knew that in mining areas there were many who still didn't think much of her, to put it mildly.

'It was all a long time ago now, wasn't it?' Sam inquired.

'You're right,' Gerry admitted. 'It was. But the passing years do not make me any fonder of the late unlamented Iron Lady.'

'Have you lived here long?' Sam asked, desperate for a change of subject.

'Twenty-five years,' Rhoda said promptly. 'Twenty-five years in the sun — and look what it's done to me!' she added. 'Some days I feel like an old lizard.'

'You have nothing at all to worry about,' Sam assured her. 'You look absolutely wonderful, Rhoda. I just hope the climate here suits me as well as it obviously does you.'

'Thank you, my dear. Can we be friends for life?'

Sam laughed. Gerry rolled his eyes again, obviously a well-practised gesture.

It was true, though, Sam thought. Rhoda did look wonderfully well and healthy, far more so than her rather florid and overweight husband. So she must be doing something right. Lots of things, probably. Like not getting drunk at every opportunity. That would be a good start.

All the same, she could understand Rhoda's concern about exposure to too much sun. Already she was starting to feel as if her own skin was drying out at an alarming rate.

Sensing interest, Rhoda began to give her advice about skin care in the local environment. Gerry lost interest altogether then and drifted away at a fair speed.

When an appropriate opening appeared, Sam asked Rhoda how she knew Simon Kendrew, Georgina's partner, wondering if there was an unfortunate experience to relate.

'Oh, we just see him from time to time, at these expat gatherings. Georgina seems to think the world of him, but I can't say I do. He seems to me to be one of those shady characters who appear on the scene occasionally out here. I just hope Georgina keeps her purse strings drawn tight, and knows how to look after her money.

'Aside from that,' Rhoda added, 'he can be very rude, as I know to my cost. He once accused Denise Matthews and me of being drunk. Do you know Denise, by the way?'

Sam admitted that she did.

'Mind you,' Rhoda added thoughtfully, 'Denise probably was drunk. She usually is at these parties. She likes to let her hair down, as do many of us. Unfortunately, Simon seems to see himself as a superior being, one called upon to point out the error of our ways to those of us not quite in his league.'

That was very true, Sam thought with a smile. That was exactly how she saw Simon. She also thought Rhoda was quite right about Georgina needing to protect herself, or her valuables at least, from him. It was interesting that someone else thought him a predator.

'Do you know where Simon lives?'

'Casa Largo, doesn't he?' Rhoda said, looking puzzled.

Sam shook her head. 'He's there a lot, but . . . '

'Oh, no! That's right. I think he has a place in that tall apartment building just off the main street. Perhaps Georgina is very sensibly keeping him at arm's length after all.'

She went on to describe a building that Sam was pretty sure she had noticed, just a block or two away from the market hall.

'Oh, goodness!' Rhoda exclaimed, suddenly looking worried.

Sam spun round to see that the little dance floor had been occupied by the birthday girl, Abby, and several others, none of whom seemed to be very good at dancing, but all of whom were in extremely high spirits. Falling over threatened to be part of whatever dance they were hoping to do.

'We didn't dance like that,' Rhoda said wonderingly. 'When we were young, I mean.'

'No?' Sam said, chuckling. 'I have to say I don't either. But they are having a lot of fun, aren't they?'

Rhoda didn't seem sure about that. 'Suzy was right,' she declared. 'Abby is drunk. Poor Hugo!'

Well, possibly, Sam thought. But she wasn't the only one. Besides, perhaps Abby was only dancing so wildly and shrieking so loudly because she and Suzy were enjoying themselves so much. They really did seem to be having a splendid time.

Still, poor Hugo. He seemed quite lost, unsure how to join in, or even if he really wanted to. Without wanting to rain on anybody's parade, Sam felt she understood his dilemma perfectly. Wild partying wasn't her scene either.

17

Rhoda and Gerry ran Sam home at the end of the evening, Hugo being fully preoccupied with Abby, who by then was not in the very best of health.

'A great evening!' Gerry declared.

'Did you enjoy it, Sam?' Rhoda asked over her shoulder from the front passenger seat.

'Yes, in parts,' Sam said diplomatically, as she got out of the car.

'I know just what you mean!' Rhoda laughed and waved gaily as the car sped away.

In parts, was about right, Sam thought. It really hadn't been her sort of evening. She was either too old or too young for that sort of event. Still, it had been good to meet Rhoda and one or two other new people. Good to see Hugo again, as well.

Poor Hugo! she thought with a wry

smile. She really did like him, and she wasn't altogether sure he was capable of keeping up with Abby. The girl had certainly led him a merry dance tonight.

★　★　★

She put it all behind her the next day and concentrated on her work, and on Simon. Rhoda had given her an idea of where Simon lived. So the party had served at least one useful purpose, so far as she was concerned.

A day or two later, she went to give the building Rhoda had described the once-over. It was much as she had expected, and had vaguely remembered: a fairly modern apartment block a dozen storeys high, with shops and offices at ground level.

Just inside the entrance there was a set of mail boxes for the occupiers of the apartments. The businesses would have their own arrangements, she decided. Direct delivery, probably, as they were all at street level. But no postman would want to be climbing six or eight storeys every day to push the letter through a private door.

No 'Simon Kendrew' here, she noted with disappointment, as she studied the names on the mail boxes. No plain 'Kendrew' either. So had Rhoda got it wrong, or . . . ? Slow down, slow down, girl! Wait and see. Probably Rhoda had just got it wrong, but it was too soon to reach a definite conclusion.

* * *

Over the next couple of days, she kept a lookout for Simon at Casa Largo, without seeing him. Then one morning he arrived and went straight into the office. She continued with what she was doing, but made sure she knew where he was all morning. Frustratingly, nothing much happened. It looked like being another blank day so far as finding anything more out by him was concerned.

An elderly couple in one of the cottages liked to have a chat with her when she was passing, and on this particular morning she was especially glad when they detained her. From where she stood, she could watch the entrance to the office building while she talked to them.

'I don't know how you keep going in this heat,' Mrs Henderson from somewhere in Yorkshire said. 'I'm sure I don't. Do you know how she does it, Fred?'

'I don't,' Fred said agreeably.

Sam smiled. 'I'm doing all right so far, while the temperature stays in the low thirties, but I might have to resign in July and August.'

'What does it get to then?' Fred asked.

'They say it gets up into the forties, touching fifty even sometimes.'

'Heavens!' Mrs Henderson said.

'That's a good temperature,' Fred said with a shrewd nod. 'It beats what we get around Barnsley. Their tomatoes here must be wonderful. Grown outside, as well.'

'Oh, you and your tomatoes!' Mrs Henderson said with a sniff.

Sam laughed. She liked them both, and enjoyed their gentle humour.

'You won't get temperatures like that where you come from either,' Fred said solemnly.

'Newcastle? Why, no! You can still get snow up our way in July and August.'

They let her go then, waving her on her way with appreciative laughter.

The timing was good. Sam had just spotted Simon leaving the office and setting off to the car park. She bundled the dirty linen she had been collecting into the laundry room and hurried over to the house to grab Georgina's car key. Luckily, Georgina was not around. So there was no need for explanation.

Simon's car was still in sight when she emerged from the car park. She put her foot down and sped through the bends that led down the hill to the main road into Sao Bras.

Keeping well back, she followed Simon into town. He made straight for the building Rhoda had told her about, parked his car on the street and disappeared inside. So Rhoda had been right, she thought with satisfaction. This really must be where he lived.

She sat in her car further along the street for a few minutes, trying to work out what to do next. Was Simon's true name 'Kendrew', she wondered, or was it one of those names on the mail boxes she had examined? Or was it something else, something completely different? He didn't have to use his real name, after all.

In fact, he could be using various names, and identities. Criminals on the run were used to doing that. They knew how to get false passports and things, as well. There was no mystery about that. All it took was money, which was something the successful ones tended to have plenty of. She bet Simon had plenty of that, the way he nagged Georgina for money.

It was most likely, she decided, that he was living under a false identity. After all, if you didn't want anyone to know who you were, you wouldn't use your real name, would you? It was hard to escape the logic of that thought.

Not that it really mattered what Simon was calling himself, or why. All she wanted to do was expose him for the fraud she was sure he was, so that Georgina could get rid of him without losing everything she had worked for over the years. How, though? How was she to do that?

She wandered around the outside of the building, taking a mental note of everything she could see. There was a parking lot at the back for residents. There was also a loading bay there for business purposes. Not much else.

At the front again, she walked past a small café, a florist's shop, a patisserie, and a shop selling the most appalling shoes for women. She lingered a few moments outside the last of those, and stared aghast at the shoes. Wherever did the ideas of style come from? Back home these would have seemed awful thirty years ago. Even her granny had never worn shoes as bad as these. She moved on.

Then there was 'Bliss', whatever that was. An office of some sort, it looked like. The door was firmly closed and locked, the Venetian blinds shuttered against the sun and the eyes of the curious. Yet there were lights on inside. It wasn't as if the place was empty. Strange way to run a business. She couldn't even tell what the business was or did.

On the way back to the car, she paused to look in the window of the shoe shop again, fascinated by how horrible the shoes were. The window was absolutely jammed full of hideous little things in all sorts of shapes and colours. All little, of course, she thought, like most of the local people seemed to be. Shoes for local people, then. Definitely not for big, fat tourists, or for anyone else with big feet.

'So will it be the crocodile-skin casuals for Madam? Or the rubber waterproofs, perhaps?'

She spun round and brought a hand up to her chest with relief. 'Hugo! Where did you spring from?'

He waved an arm vaguely and said, 'I live here. Remember?'

She smiled. 'So you said. Of course you do. No, I was just admiring the local shoe styles.'

'Good?'

She shook her head and grimaced. 'I don't think so. None of these would ever be worn in Newcastle.'

'Because Newcastle is a provincial city, and behind the times fashion-wise?'

'Yes, that must be it. But just look at them!'

Hugo moved closer and peered in the window. 'I don't know much about women's shoes,' he admitted.

She laughed and clutched his arm unthinkingly. 'Now why aren't I surprised?'

'See them, though?' he added, pointing at a pair of sand-coloured casual shoes with petite bows just above the toes.

'What about them?'

'What do you think they are made of?'

'I have no idea,' she said, peering closer. 'It's not leather, though, is it?'

'Cork.'

'What?'

'They're made of cork, a local speciality. The stuff that goes in wine bottles.'

'I do know what cork is, Hugo. Hm. Interesting. I had no idea you could do things like that with cork.'

She studied the shoes a little longer, but whatever they were made of, she decided, they were not shoes she would ever be wearing.

'Come on!' Hugo added. 'Let me buy you a coffee.'

18

They went once again to the little café in the market that Sam was coming to know so well. She liked it there. The owners and staff were very friendly and helpful, and she enjoyed the way they treated her as an honoured guest now, the friend of their friend Hugo. This time was no different. They were besieged by good-humoured people eager to tell Hugo the latest and to provide for them the very best coffee in Sao Bras.

'It's a matter of principle,' Hugo told her when he eventually sat down alongside her. 'Pedro's grandfather started this café, and they have always been proud of their coffee here.'

'Low prices, too?' Sam asked with a smile.

'That, too,' Hugo agreed. He smiled. 'It's good to see you, Sam!'

'Why, thank you!' she said with a smile, and with some surprise. 'Tell me, Hugo, have you recovered from the party yet?'

'Just about,' he said with a grimace.

'Abby, too?'

'I don't know.' He shrugged and added, 'Maybe. I haven't spoken to her since. I haven't had the chance.'

'She was all right that night, I assume? I mean ... well, all right, basically?'

He shrugged. Then he grinned and said, 'Abby is a law unto herself. She copes pretty well with whatever happens.'

Sam smiled. 'I think everyone enjoyed themselves that evening. Suzy must have been well pleased they gave her such a fine celebration.'

'Yes, you're right.'

Hugo frowned and seemed stuck for something to say for a moment. Sam smiled inwardly. She knew it hadn't been his kind of thing, any more than it had been hers.

'It got a bit wild towards the end?' she suggested.

'As usual,' Hugo admitted with a sheepish grin. 'People here have a way of partying. Not the Portuguese — the English, the Brits. It must be something to do with the heat.'

'And the free-flowing wine?'

'That, too!'

'I met a very nice couple from Rotherham, Rhoda and Gerry. They gave me a lift home.'

'Yes?'

'You know them, I assume?'

He nodded without much interest.

'But I didn't meet Suzy's father, who I gather threw the party.'

'No. He wasn't there. He seldom is. He's like Abby's father. Both of them are always flying off here or there on business. Hong Kong one week. New York another.'

'Oh? What do they do?'

'No idea.' He shook his head. 'Abby doesn't seem to know either. They are both millionaires anyway. Sao Bras isn't good enough to detain them for long, but it's good enough for them to park their daughters here while they visit the world's hotspots.'

Clearly, Hugo didn't approve of their lifestyle. Perhaps that was to do with Abby. It sounded like another poor-little-rich-girl story.

'What do their wives say about it?'

Hugo shook his head. 'Neither of them has a wife any more. Abby's mum died, and Suzy's parents are divorced.'

Sam began to wonder if all that had had anything to do with Hugo and Abby getting together. She could well imagine that it had. Both had experienced parental loss at a relatively young age.

Otherwise, she couldn't see that they had a lot in common. Abby didn't seem the right sort of woman for Hugo. Well, who would be? she thought. Me? She smiled inwardly at that. Chance would be a fine thing, as her mother was inclined to say.

'How did you and Abby meet?' she asked.

'Simon introduced us,' Hugo said with another of his shrugs.

She stared, almost open-mouthed, but no further information was forthcoming.

* * *

As she walked back to the car afterwards, Sam bumped into Randolph.

'*Boa noite*, Randolph!' Good evening.

He stopped and peered hard at her. 'My dear! *Boa noite* to you too. Spoken like a true native. How quickly you've learned the language.'

She laughed. 'That's a quarter of my vocabulary, Randolph!'

'Every journey starts with the first step. You have taken that step. So, to what do I owe the pleasure of seeing you this evening?'

'A bit of shopping I had to do. That's all, I'm afraid. Nothing glamorous. But

I've just had coffee with Hugo. I met him in the street. It's becoming a habit, I'm afraid.'

'Did you go to Pedro's?'

'Yes, we did. Hugo says it's the best coffee in the town.'

Randolph thought for a moment before saying, 'Not quite, perhaps, now. But good enough.'

'Oh, Randolph! You're an old perfectionist. The coffee there is lovely.'

'But not quite as good as when the old man had the café. Now I seldom go there. You and Hugo must find a lot to talk about?'

It was a strange thing to say, but Sam nodded. 'He's good company. I like him.'

'Has he told you about his painting?'

'Who? Hugo?'

'Indeed.'

'He paints, does he? No, he's not mentioned that. Is he good?'

'Well . . . Painting amuses him, I think. Good? I hardly think so. All right, shall we say, for a young man living in such a benighted place as our little town.'

Goodness! she thought. That's scarcely a ringing endorsement. How unkind of Randolph to put it like that.

'Well, I'm all in favour of people exercising any creative talent they have. I only wish I had some. What does he paint?'

'Oh, the usual,' Randolph said vaguely. 'Hills and olive trees.'

Then he waved an apologetic hand and announced that he must be off. A student would be waiting for him.

Sam had the distinct impression that he regretted having mentioned Hugo's interest in painting. And she wondered why nobody, not Randolph or Georgina or Hugo himself, had ever mentioned it before. Modesty, perhaps, on Hugo's part. But Randolph? Why had he been so curmudgeonly?

19

Sam took the mail the delivery man handed her and went into the office to sort through it, as she sometimes did when Georgina was not around. There was quite a bit for Casa Largo, and for Georgina herself, mostly payments by the look of the envelopes. Always good to see!

Then she frowned and studied an envelope addressed to a Mr Bliss. There was no-one here with that name, and she had seen other mail previously with that name. Odd. Why would the postman continue bringing them here? Some envelopes were simply addressed to '*Mr Bliss, Sao Bras*'. It was strange. They needed to have a word with the postman, or with the post office in town.

Just then the door opened and Simon walked in.

'Hi, Sam! Is that the mail you have there?'

'Hello, Simon. Yes. It's just arrived. Some of it seems to be misdirected. I was just going to . . .'

Simon moved in front of her, glanced at the envelopes spread on the shelf and said, 'These shouldn't be here.'

'No, I . . .'

'I'll sort them. Best, in fact, if you just leave the mail to me or Georgina in future. We know what to do with it. OK?'

Sam shrugged and moved aside, annoyed to be dismissed in such an off-hand way. Sorting out the mail was the office junior's job in any office where she had ever worked. It was no big deal.

As she left, she suddenly recalled seeing the name Bliss somewhere else: above the office window in the building where Simon lived. Bliss. Was that another of Simon's names? Was that yet another name of convenience?

It was no coincidence, she decided,

that mail marked 'Bliss' had been delivered here. There must be some sort of connection between Simon, that building and mail arriving here. She wondered what it was. She wondered that a lot. Perhaps that office, that business, was part of some illicit enterprise Simon was running? She wouldn't be at all surprised.

Just then she caught sight of Esmeralda, the girl from the nearby village who came in to help when things at Casa Largo were particularly hectic.

'*Bom dia*, Esmeralda! How are you today?'

The girl replied with her usual beaming smile. 'Sam! Hello. Me? I am very fine, thank you. It is a lovely day, no?'

'Wonderful,' Sam agreed.

Esmeralda did not have a lot of English, nor Sam much Portuguese, and between them by then they had pretty well exhausted their joint vocabulary. But Sam still had the encounter with Simon on her mind, and decided to try a little more conversation. Besides, she liked the girl, who was a very hard worker and unfailingly pleasant to have around. Georgina was lucky to have her on call, and Sam wanted to encourage her to keep coming here.

'Esmeralda, do you go into Sao Bras a lot? Very often, I mean?'

The girl considered the question, working through the meaning. Then she brightened and said, '*Sim!* Yes! Often I go, for my father's medicine.'

'How do you go? There isn't a bus, is there?'

'Bus? No, no bus. Only one day bus.'

One day a week, Sam realised she meant.

'So how do you go? Walk?'

Esmeralda shook her head. 'I go by brother's . . . ' She broke off to mime how she travelled.

'Ah! You go by bicycle?'

'*Sim.* You wish to borrow bicycle?'

Sam shook her head, and wondered if it was worth trying to prolong the conversation. It was so difficult when neither of them had more than a smattering of the other's language, and her own knowledge of Portuguese was less than a smattering. Esmeralda was wonderfully bilingual by comparison.

'Do you know the high building where Simon lives?'

She mimed, too, somehow managing to convey what she meant.

Esmeralda nodded. '*Sim*,' she said again. 'Mr Simon lives there.'

'There is an office there at ground level, a shop perhaps, called Bliss. Do you know it?'

'Bliss? Yes, I know.' Esmeralda broke into a surprising smile. 'Mr Simon,' she added. 'Mr Simon, Mr Bliss. Yes?'

What was she saying? Sam wondered.

'In that building where Simon lives, there is a business called Bliss. Do you know what it is?'

Esmeralda shrugged and looked doubtful. It was hard to tell whether her uncertainty was about the question or the answer.

'We get mail here at Casa Largo that is addressed to Mr Bliss,' Sam tried hopefully. 'Do you know why?'

'Yes, yes,' Esmeralda said, smiling again. 'Mr Simon, Mr Bliss.'

At that point, Sam gave up. There seemed little point pursuing the conversation further.

She changed the subject. 'Esmeralda, has Georgina said we would like you to come here again on Saturday?'

'Saturday? Yes. And Mr Bliss?'

'Oh, Esmeralda!' she said despairingly. 'Please forget I ever mentioned it.'

They exchanged smiles and parted. It was only when Sam was cleaning the next cottage that she thought of something. Surely the girl had not been saying that Mr Bliss and Mr Simon were the same person? Surely not?

20

'Sam, would you mind meeting the Entwhistles yourself this morning?' Georgina asked over breakfast. 'I've got such a lot to sort out in the office. Simon can't be here today.'

'No, that's not a problem. They're coming at twelve, aren't they?'

'That's what they said. They stayed overnight in Faro, and were going to hire a car there to travel up here.'

Sam did a quick mental inventory of the work to be done and decided it was all possible still.

'You know, Georgina, I would be quite happy to help out in the office if you need any help there.'

'Oh, there's so much to do! I don't think I could even begin to explain things.'

'Well, I'm sure I could soon catch on. I've worked in offices all my life. It's what I do. Normally, that is. I'm a trained accountant.'

Georgina looked doubtful, as if she feared Casa Largo's accounting systems would prove too much even for the Bank of England's accountant.

'Well,' Sam said, 'I don't want to push my way in, but the offer's there — if you ever need it.'

'That's very sweet of you, Sam. Thank you. I shall remember that if we have an emergency. Now, more tea?'

Sam gave an inward smile and wondered if Georgina had avoided grabbing her hand off because of the state of her books. Perhaps she didn't want the unfortunate truth to be revealed.

In contemplative mood now, Georgina confided, 'I don't know how I'd manage without Simon. He's a rock. It's such a pity he can't be here today. He would soon sort the paperwork out.'

'He's busy, is he?'

'Hm?' Georgina said. 'Oh, yes. He is. Very busy, unfortunately.'

Doing what? Sam wondered. Working on his criminal enterprises?

'What does he do when he's not here? Does he have a job?'

'A business,' Georgina said.

'Oh? What kind of business?'

Georgina shrugged. 'You know,' she said vaguely. 'Some sort of business. I'm not exactly sure what it is, but it keeps him very busy.'

'To do with money?' Sam asked, chancing her arm.

'I'm not really sure.'

Recently, Sam had read about foreigners in the Algarve who practised loan sharking, money lending at exorbitant rates of interest, sometimes followed up by acts of violence on those who couldn't or wouldn't pay. She wouldn't be at all surprised, she thought now, if Simon was into that sort of business. It would fit very well with what she knew of the man.

'How long have you known Simon?'

'Two or three years, I suppose. I can't remember exactly. I just know I couldn't do without him,' Georgina finished with a wan smile.

Sam flinched inwardly. Poor Georgina. She really was in a sad state if that was the case.

Loan sharking, she thought again. That would fit very well. Simon would be good at pushing people around and fleecing them when they were financially vulnerable. Like Georgina herself? Yes, exactly. Randolph had told her the finances at Casa Largo were shaky, and she had heard Simon demanding money from Georgina. Loan sharking could very well be at the bottom of it.

It probably wasn't a love match at all between Georgina and Simon. It was a shameful business deal that poor Georgina couldn't escape. That's what it must be. Heavens! He could even be angling to take over Casa Largo.

Well, they would see about that, she thought grimly. She was not going to allow Simon to get away with it. Somehow she was going to put a stop to whatever it was he was up to.

★　★　★

A day or two later, Sam returned to what she now thought of as the 'Bliss Building', the high-rise block where Simon lived. Nothing had changed. It looked exactly the same, as she wandered around the outside and then checked the mail boxes on the inside again.

Back outside, all the shops were open and doing business, all, that is, apart from the Bliss office itself. That was still closed and locked, the blinds shut tight. There seemed no possibility of a customer getting inside, even in the unlikely event of one ever appearing on the doorstep. Perhaps it was some sort of tax dodge? Some way of writing off taxes against a pretend business.

She shrugged and turned away. Who could tell? She crossed the street and entered a small patisserie. Feeling frustrated, she ordered a coffee and quite a large sticky bun. She had to have something to take away the frustration of having made no progress on the Simon case. She was no further forward at all. Staring across the street at the Bliss Building, she felt like taking a tin opener to it, and spilling all its secrets into the street. What on earth was Simon Kendrew up to?

Money laundering was one possibility. That was something else she had read about. But increasingly she believed it was probably loan sharking. That was what fit the facts she knew best. She stirred her coffee slowly, eyes narrowed in concentration as she stared across the street at the Bliss Building.

Then she jerked upright and stared with shock. He had just arrived. Simon. He was here!

She watched as he got out of his car, slammed the door shut and then pulled a bunch of keys out of his pocket. She held her breath and waited, wondering what would come next. To her astonishment, Simon approached the door to the Bliss office, inserted a key, unlocked the door, and marched inside. The door banged shut behind him.

With difficulty, she refrained from jumping up and rushing across the street to pound on the door of Bliss and demand entry. Instead, she sat and thought. And she remembered what Esmeralda had so improbably seemed to be saying: Mr Simon is Mr Bliss. At the time she had dismissed the idea. But now she realised Esmeralda had quite possibly been right.

★ ★ ★

'Do you know the Bliss office across the street?' she asked the middle-aged man behind the counter of the café while she was waiting for another coffee.

He peered across the street and nodded. 'I see it,' he assured her. 'I see it every day.'

He got to work then on the machine that poured steam through the coffee and made it froth up as if it were in a volcanic cauldron. Sam waited patiently for the noise level to drop.

'What is it, that business?'

He considered the question for a long moment. Then he shrugged. 'Who knows?'

'It's never open,' Sam persisted. 'Every day I see it, but always the door is locked and there are no customers. I just wondered what their business was.'

'Maybe they are bankrupt,' the man suggested without much interest.

That was a possibility she had not considered.

'Maybe it is something illegal?' she suggested mischievously.

'Oh, yes!' the man said, nodding wisely. 'It is clear to me that you are a very intelligent person.'

Was that a Portuguese put-down?

'I like your coffee,' she said with a smile.

'Like all intelligent people,' he said without a hint of a smile. Then, 'This one is free.'

'Thank you,' she said.

'You are most welcome. Computers.'

'I beg your pardon?'

'Bliss. Something to do with computers, I believe.'

21

Computers, she thought as she walked away. Bliss and computers. Simon and computers? Could he have something to do with them? Maybe.

White collar crime, then? Possibly. She still liked loan sharking or money laundering, but she would keep an open mind. The café proprietor was no fool. If he said something to do with computers, it was worth taking note.

That Simon! She would get him in the end. She would. She was determined.

*   *   *

She was cleaning up the barbecue area when Hugo appeared, a big smile on his face.

'Hi, Sam.'

'Hello, Hugo! What are you doing here?'

'I just came to see Mum. But I seem to have missed her.'

'You have. She's gone to Loule to do a bit of shopping.'

'Spending money? It's not like her.'

Sam chuckled. 'Your mother works extremely hard. She's entitled to a bit of occasional retail recreation.'

'Is that what you call it?'

'It is where I come from.'

He grinned. 'So how are you today?'

'Hot. I've just about finished up here. Have you got time for a lemonade or a coffee?'

'Plenty of time. I've got nothing on this morning.'

'You can give us a hand then. We always can use extra hands.'

'Don't I know it,' Hugo admitted. 'I told Mum I'd be happy to help out when needed, but not work here every day any more. I think that's when you came in — I freed up an employment opportunity.'

'Well, thank you very much! Come on. Let's retire to the kitchen.'

It was cool there, in the kitchen, cool and peaceful. The windows were placed to catch the early morning light, but the sun had moved on now, leaving the room no more than pleasantly warm.

'Lemonade or coffee?' Sam queried. 'Or both?'

'Both would be good.'

She took the jug from the fridge and poured two glasses of Georgina's home-made lemonade while she waited for the kettle to boil.

'You must have sat at this table so many times over the years, Hugo.'

'Every day of my life nearly,' he admitted with a wry smile.

'Does it still feel like home?'

'Of course.' He looked around and added, 'I could close my eyes a continent away from here and describe every detail of this room. It hasn't changed.'

Sam smiled. 'Home, then. But you're enjoying life in town?'

He nodded. 'Mum is wonderful, and I love her dearly, but I needed to get away on my own. I have things I want to do. Besides, she and Simon need space and time to be on their own, too.'

'I'm not sure about that, Hugo. Anyway, what do you do with all this spare time you've acquired? Oh, I know! You paint, don't you? Randolph told me.'

He shrugged, a reluctant tacit admission.

'Do you spend much time painting?'

'I paint part of every day. Most days, at least. It's what I like to do.'

'Is that why you wanted to get away from here?'

'Yes, it is. I needed to be able to think and concentrate on what I was doing, without feeling guilty about neglecting all the work that always needs doing on the cottages. Now I just do technical stuff here, like sorting out the televisions and mending important things that break. Like windows,' he added with a smile.

'What does your mum think about it all?'

'She's in two minds, I think. She was impatient at first, and understandably resentful that I was leaving her with so much to do. But she also knew I had to lead my own life, and do what interested me.'

'So she came round?'

He shrugged. 'Maybe. I don't know.'

She would have liked to ask him more about Simon, as well, but it seemed too soon. She was enjoying the moment, sitting here with him, talking to him. She didn't want it to end any time soon.

He was so fine-looking, and so lovely in his ways. She liked him very much. What a pity he had a girlfriend! Stop it, she told herself. Just stop it.

Besides, he wasn't interested in her in that way. He was just a lovely man who would be unfailingly pleasant with everyone he met. That's what he was like. She wasn't special to him, as he was in danger of becoming to her.

'What kind of painting do you do?' she asked. 'I mean, is it fiercely modern and impossible for someone like me to understand, or . . . '

'Or popular rubbish?' Hugo suggested playfully.

'No! Of course not,' she said hastily, feeling herself colour with embarrassment.

'Why don't you come and see for yourself?' he suggested. 'I'm not good at talking about what I do.'

'I would like that, Hugo.'

'Then come tomorrow. How's that?'

'Thank you. I will.'

★   ★   ★

She shivered with anticipation later when she thought about it. Hugo's invitation had come out of nowhere. She certainly hadn't expected it, nor had she been angling for it. But it did delight her.

As well as an opportunity to see more, and learn more, about Hugo, it might be an opportunity to get to grips with him about Simon. Perhaps tomorrow she would find out at last what was going on at Casa Largo. That was something else she looked forward to very much.

But not as much, she had to admit with a wry smile, as simply spending a little time with Hugo.

★   ★   ★

Early that evening Sam visited a café she knew was popular with some of the younger people who had been at Suzy's party. She wasn't entirely sure why she found herself heading in that direction, but she knew it had something to do with Hugo. It also had something to do with Simon Kendrew. Bliss, too, perhaps? Perhaps.

She was in luck. Suzy was there, and sitting all alone too, although glances at her watch suggested that wouldn't be for long.

'Waiting for someone special?'

Suzy looked up, startled. 'Oh, hello Sam! What are you doing here?'

'I do get off work sometimes, you know.'

Suzy laughed. 'Lucky you! I'm just waiting for Abby and a couple of the other girls. We're going to have a girls' night out. Do you want to join us?'

'No, thank you! I'm far too old for that sort of thing. I wouldn't last the pace.'

'Of course you would.'

Sam shook her head firmly.

She ordered a Coke and sat down at Suzy's table. By then, Suzy was engrossed in something on her smart phone. Sam didn't interrupt her. She waited patiently until Suzy switched off and looked up.

'Sorry,' Suzy said. 'Just keeping up with everyone.'

Sam grinned. 'Full-time job?'

'Just about!'

'Do you all live here in town?'

'Most of us do. No point living out in the sticks, is there? Abby's dad has a house near Font de Pedra. Do you know that area?'

Sam nodded.

'And I live with my dad on that new estate on the east side of town.'

'Do you like it there?'

'It's all right, for now. Maybe next year I'll move on, get my own place. I might even leave and go to London. Somewhere there's more happening.'

Sam nodded, thinking she wouldn't know what hit her if she did. Small town life in Portugal was no preparation for London. On the other hand, Suzy was very young. That made a difference. The young could usually cope.

'I've bumped into Hugo a few times,' she said. 'He lives in town, as well, doesn't he?'

'Yeah. He's got a flat. Don't know where, though.'

Suzy shrugged and added, 'He's a nice guy, Hugo, but not exactly my idea of . . . ' She shrugged again and came to a stop.

'I wouldn't have thought he was exactly Abby's either!'

Suzy grinned. 'That's true.'

'I wondered how they met. Hugo said Simon introduced them.'

'That's true. He did. Oh, look!' she said, glancing at her phone. 'I was waiting for this call. Do you mind?'

Sam shook her head, smiled and got up. 'I'll leave you to it.'

She wondered whether to order a coffee and wait until the phone call was finished, but a call Suzy had been waiting for might last forever. Her mind was finally made up when she spotted Abby and a couple of other girls crossing the street. Time to go!

She waved to Abby as she left the café and turned to her left to walk away. She didn't want to risk being roped in for a girls' night out. That was the last thing she wanted.

'Coming, Sam?' Abby called after her.

'No thanks! Enjoy yourselves.'

They must be desperately short of

numbers to invite me, she thought with a smile as she walked away. And once again she wondered what on earth Hugo and Abby found they had in common. Don't ask! she thought with another smile.

Then she frowned as she remembered that Suzy had confirmed what Hugo himself had told her. Hugo and Abby had met through Simon. How odd was that?

22

Finding Hugo's flat wasn't easy. In fact, in the end she had to resort to phoning him.

'Hello, Hugo. Shamefully, I have to tell you I'm lost!'

He chuckled. 'You found the Chinese furniture store?'

'I managed that.' She glanced behind her at the window full of gigantic ceramic pots, urns, or whatever they were, and added, 'It would be hard to miss this shop.'

Hugo gave her some very precise directional instructions that required her to cross the road, enter what looked like a private garden via a green wooden gate, then . . . steps, stairs, white gateway, tall cactus . . . Until she was there.

'At last!' she said when she saw him standing in an open doorway waiting for her.

'At last,' he confirmed with a big smile. 'Welcome!'

★　★　★

Like Randolph's place, it was a big flat. There were several rooms in addition to kitchen and bathroom. Most were no doubt intended to be bedrooms, but now one was a workshop or studio and another was a display gallery. Or something. Sam looked around with fascination. Paintings everywhere. The walls were not big enough to carry them all. Big, vividly coloured paintings of hills and rocks and forests.

'Hugo! I had no idea.' She flapped a hand in astonishment. 'All this!'

'Coffee?'

'What?' she asked, dazed by the torrents of colour forcing themselves on her from all sides.

'Let's have a cup of coffee first. Then you can poke around, and see if you like anything.'

'Oh, Hugo! I'm overwhelmed already.

198

How have you found the time to do all this?'

'Principally, by leaving Casa Largo to you and Mum,' he said simply.

*   *   *

They took cups of coffee out on to a broad balcony facing west, where they could sit in the evening sunshine and gaze out across the town to the hills beyond. It was quiet, peaceful. Vines growing in big terracotta pots had draped themselves overhead and wrapped around the wrought-iron railings at the edge of the balcony.

'You have a lovely flat, Hugo. However did you find it?'

'Through friends,' he said with a shrug. 'Somebody's aunt's friend had a nephew who knew someone with a flat to rent. The owner's wife liked me — possibly too much,' he added with a grin. 'So she persuaded her husband to lower the rent to a price I could afford. Like that.'

'Like that,' she repeated, amused.

'It suits me here,' he added, glancing around.

She nodded. It would suit her, too. He had been lucky to get it.

'I saw Suzy a little while ago,' she said. 'She was waiting for Abby and some other friends.'

Hugo smiled. 'They are always doing something, or going somewhere. They lead busy lives, those girls.'

But not you? She found herself thinking, but didn't say.

'Show me around your gallery, Hugo.'

Most of Hugo's paintings were landscapes in oils. They were big pictures, displaying vast panoramas in vivid colours that took your breath away. Some were of ranges of wooded hills, such as were to be found north of Sao Bras. Others were of sea cliffs and rocky crags. Then there were the historic townscapes, and also a few lively modern street scenes that Sam guessed were of Faro.

'Where's this?' she asked, pointing at a blood-red castle labouring under a fierce sun.

'That is in Silves, the town the Moors made their capital of the Algarve. It's on a river, a few miles inland from Portimao. They were safe there from attack from the sea, or so they thought, and yet could still import what they needed and export their dried fruit and nuts, their wheat and textiles.'

'What happened?'

'Oh, lots of things. It wasn't as safe as they imagined it to be. Pirates and Crusaders found it from time to time, and besieged it. Sometimes the siege failed. Sometimes it prevailed. And the river silted up badly. The town is still there, intact, but no longer the capital,' he concluded.

'I would like to see it sometime.'

He nodded. 'It is interesting. You would like it, I think.'

'And this? Where is this?'

'Rocha da Pena, not too far from here. It's a table mountain, and again was a favoured site historically. On the summit there are Neolithic defence works.'

So many places, Sam thought, as they moved on. So many hills and buildings, towns and rivers. And so wonderfully painted. The colours were gorgeous, whether they were vibrant or tranquil.

'I can't believe all this, Hugo. Your paintings are wonderful. And I can't believe nobody told me you were an artist until recently. What does Randolph say about your work?'

'Randolph?' Hugo smiled. 'Randolph doesn't believe what I do is art. I'm not an artist in his eyes.'

'Oh? Why on earth not?'

'I didn't go to art school. I am untaught. And I paint landscapes, not abstract patterns like him. So I am an untrained primitive in his eyes. All that is true,' he finished with a shrug.

'Well, I don't really understand that attitude. I think you're a fine painter, Hugo. I know next to nothing about art, but coming in here was an overwhelming experience. I don't think you should worry at all what Randolph thinks.'

'I don't. I just go my own way, impervious to his opinions and criticisms. That, of course, is another reason for criticism.'

Hugo smiled, gave her a little bow and said, 'But thank you, Sam. I appreciate your advice, and your kind words.'

23

Back at the kitchen table, this time with a glass of cool white wine, Sam said, 'Ever thought of doing this full-time, Hugo? Making a living out of your painting?'

'All the time!' Hugo said, grinning.

'Oh! Of course.' The penny dropped. 'That's why you don't have a regular job?'

He nodded. 'I do casual work, when I can. Anything that helps keep the wolf from the door. It's not much of a living, but I manage somehow. And I keep painting.

'That was why I was so determined to get away from Casa Largo. When I was there, I had no time for painting. A half-hour here, and another there, isn't enough. I needed more than that. I don't think Mum ever really understood that. So she was disappointed when I pulled out.'

He shrugged and added, 'But it had to happen. Casa Largo is her baby, but this is mine.'

'So how are you doing now? Are you selling your work?'

'Well, one or two pictures. That's all. I'm not making much money, and I may not be able to keep going like this forever, but for now I'm happy. I'm painting. I'm doing what I wanted to do. Eventually, I suppose, I might have to give up and get a job. I hope not, but . . .'

'I hope you don't either,' Sam said quickly. 'What you are doing here is wonderful, Hugo. You should keep at it.'

She thought for a moment and added, 'Randolph said finances were a problem at Casa Largo, too. Is that right, do you think?'

Hugo shrugged. 'Probably. But going back there full-time is not an option anyway. Simon and I don't get on terribly well. Besides, I'm not going to stop painting, however much he thinks it's a waste of time.'

'Quite right, too,' Sam said decisively. 'You shouldn't even think of that.'

'I think Mum has the same opinion as Simon, actually,' Hugo added. 'I don't suppose she thinks what I'm trying to do is worthwhile either, not when there are so many things at Casa Largo crying out for attention.'

'Ignore them both,' Sam said firmly. 'Don't take any notice of them.'

Ignore Simon especially, she thought. If I have anything to do with it, he's not going to be around much longer anyway. I'm going to expose him for the fraud he is. Then we'll get rid of him.

* * *

On the way home, Sam found herself thinking again how much she liked Hugo. He was a lovely man. So talented too. What a pity he was spoken for! Abby probably didn't realise how lucky she was. But the young were like that, weren't they? She had been herself. It was only afterwards that you realised what a good thing you had so carelessly thrown away.

Not that that would happen here. There was no reason at all for it. Good luck to them both. They were a lovely couple, and she wished them well.

She also really did hope Hugo could find a way of making a living from his art. That would be a wonderful thing. Surely it must be possible?

So many of the paintings she had seen were absolutely wonderful. She couldn't be the only person in the world who felt like that. Surely there were people out there who would buy Hugo's paintings, given the chance? There had to be.

Forget Georgina and Simon, and their lack of interest. Forget Randolph, too, and his carping criticism. The world had moved on since Randolph's time in art school. Hugo should just continue down his own path. She was sure he would be able to sell his pictures if he could only get organised.

Was there any way, she wondered, that she could find to help him? Maybe. It was worth thinking about. Hugo might be able to paint, but he obviously had no idea of business and marketing. She would have to put her thinking cap on and see if there was anything she could do to help.

* * *

For the moment, she had quite forgotten about Simon, so long such a preoccupation for her. That changed when she got back to Casa Largo and found Georgina and Simon together, both of them looking particularly happy.

'Join us for a glass of wine?' Simon suggested.

'A celebratory glass of wine!' Georgina added.

That was the last thing Sam felt like doing. She could scarcely bear to be in the same room as Simon. But it would have been so ungracious to turn

Georgina down that she felt she had no choice.

'Celebratory?' she said as she sat down with them on the terrace. 'What? Have we got a block booking? Won the Lottery?'

'Nothing like that,' Georgina said. 'Tell her,' she said happily to Simon.

Simon gave a little smile and said, 'Georgina and I are to be married, Sam. She has done me the honour of accepting my proposal this evening, and you are the first to know.'

Sam stared, incredulous. What horror! The last thing she had expected. The last thing she had wanted, too. What on earth was wrong with Georgina?'

'How lovely,' she said as calmly as she could manage. 'Congratulations.'

It sounded a bit flat. Perhaps Georgina had anticipated her jumping in the air and screeching with delight. Well, she wasn't going to do that. She couldn't.

She knew now she had to speed up

her efforts to unmask Simon Kendrew. Time was running out, if a disaster of enormous proportions was to be averted. Georgina's life would be ruined if this went ahead, and with it Hugo's too, probably. There was no time to spare, none at all.

'When is it to be?' she asked.

'Soon,' Georgina said, 'as soon as possible. Neither of us is getting any younger, and we have no reason to wait a moment longer.'

Oh, yes you do! Sam thought. You just don't know it yet. She felt more depressed, but more determined, than ever.

24

Despite everything going on with Simon, and now with Georgina as well, Sam couldn't help puzzling away at what she could do to help Hugo. There must be something. What might it be?

She admitted she had no idea if Hugo's paintings were great art or not, but that didn't seem to matter. What was great art anyway? All the modern artists of renown she heard and read about seemed to be doing things like stuffing sharks and exhibiting their unmade bed as art. She was sure she wouldn't be the only person in the world who preferred Hugo's beautiful paintings.

Also, there were plenty of people these days who were able to afford to buy things they liked and display them in their own homes, despite the economy. Just think about the tat so many people did have! An original oil painting was in a different class altogether. She might even get Mum one for Christmas. It was worth thinking about.

Then there was the souvenir trade. Lots of people who came to the Algarve would be taking all sorts of things home with them as mementoes of a wonderful holiday in the sun. Why couldn't some of those things be pictures? Why not original art? Oh, there were all sorts of possibilities when you thought about it. It was no good being timid. You had to get out there and interest people, display and sell your work.

How could someone like Hugo go about that? Well, first you needed a shop, a gallery. Somewhere your pictures could be seen, with price labels. Or, for a superior class of art like she thought Hugo's paintings were, the pictures could be on display but the prices might be more discreetly advertised in a glossy catalogue. Something like that.

She couldn't immediately think of anywhere in Sao Bras that would make a suitable place for exhibiting Hugo's art. Craft products perhaps, but not original oil paintings. The town was too small and workmanlike, and the wealthy visitors too few. They would probably be better off going further afield, to a bigger town with many more potential clients.

The more she thought about it, the more sure she was that that conclusion was correct. Right, then, she decided, I can help with that. I can roll up my sleeves and make a start. Why not?

Faro, the modern capital of the Algarve, seemed the obvious place to go. She discussed her ideas with Hugo, who agreed without much confidence but left it to her. Then, when she next had a day off, she borrowed Georgina's car again and set off for Faro.

In the car boot she had half a dozen of Hugo's paintings, a mixed bag to show the range of his work. She also had good photos of them and other pictures on her smart phone. She had even printed out a few of the photos on cards. Hopefully, she had enough with her to make a start and persuade somebody to take an interest.

* * *

Easier said than done was a phrase that soon came to mind. There were one or two shops stocking art and craft items for sale down near the marina, but the staff in them were uninterested in what Sam had to say once they realised she was not a customer. Disconsolately, she wandered the streets in the search for somewhere more likely.

The manager in one little place was interested in hearing her out, and even offered her a cup of coffee, but sadly was unable to offer any practical help.

'We take only work from students at the university,' the man explained. 'It is . . . what? A contract! That's it. I am sorry not to be able to help you.'

Sam thanked him and left.

She walked away from the marina, and along towards the end of the promenade. It grew increasingly windy along there and more uncomfortable, and also even less promising. The shops petered out. Huge planes flew just over her head, and skimmed the castle too, as they took off from the nearby airport and soared out over the ocean. The Atlantic, she reminded herself moodily. This was not the Mediterranean, however blue the sea.

An old timber building on the seaward side of the road, that had once been something else, had been renovated in recent years and now allegedly functioned as a dance studio. Illustrations of the dance styles on offer to potential students were displayed on painted boards beside and over the doorway. Salsa and flamingo, tango and bebop, lindy hop even, were just a few of the dance courses on offer. No waltzes and foxtrots anymore, though. It was a studio, a school, for the likes of Abby and Suzy, not for older people with time on their hands.

Sam smiled and moved on, skirting a couple of big gulls that had salvaged something to eat from the bins behind a café. Gulls were not big on fish. They seemed to like their meals to be wrapped in paper bags or old newspaper. Fish and chips was what they liked best at home. Or the remains of a hamburger or a kebab. That sort of thing.

Suddenly she paused, as a new thought struck her. With a frown, she turned and went back to look at the illustrations on the boards outside the dance studio again. She studied them for a couple of minutes. Then she headed inside.

A large woman with masses of unruly curly red hair was in the reception area, pointing and gesticulating, laughing and ordering people about in high good humour. It all seemed to be taken in good part.

'What's it going to be, pet?' the

woman demanded, turning to Sam. 'Learn the tango for the boyfriend, or jazz dancing to get rid of some of that excess weight?'

Sam was astonished, and mildly outraged. 'You talking to me, hinny?' she demanded. 'Who do you think you are, with your high-falutin' ways? Cushy Butterfield?'

In her turn, the red-haired woman stared open-mouthed for a moment. Then she threw back her head and roared with laughter. 'Well, I never!' she exclaimed. 'What's a nice Geordie woman like yourself doing in a place like this?'

'I could ask you the same question,' Sam pointed out with a smile. It had been a lovely surprise to hear the familiar accent.

'Oh, I've been here many a year. Fell out of a plane, I think. Onto my head, probably. Like a coffee?'

'Love one.'

'Come on, then. This lot can manage without me for a few minutes,' she added, waving a hand at her grinning and perhaps bemused staff.

★ ★ ★

Jessie Robson, she said her name was. And, yes, it was her studio. Not an absolutely great life here, perhaps, but one a lot better than she could have expected when she was growing up in Felling, on the south bank of the Tyne.

'You'll be from the other side of the water, yourself?' she added.

Sam smiled. 'You've got a good ear for accents! Yes, Newcastle. Fenham, actually.'

'The posh part?'

'Not really. Not where we live.'

Jessie poured the coffee, sat down and said, 'You're not really here to learn how to dance, are you?'

Sam shook her head. 'Sorry. I'm not. I was admiring the illustrations at the front of the studio when it suddenly occurred to me that you might be able to help me. Do you know people in the arts world here in Faro?'

'A few. What is it you're after?'

Sam took a few minutes to explain, saying that basically she had a friend who was looking for a gallery, or something similar, that might be interested in displaying some of his paintings.

'What kind of paintings?'

Sam took out her phone and began to show the photos of Hugo's pictures she had stored there.

'Portuguese, Algarve, landscapes, mostly. He lives in Sao Bras de Apportel, and has lived there all his life.'

'And you're his agent? Or what? Is he your feller, perhaps?'

'Not really. I'm working for his mother at her guesthouse for the season. I just thought I would see if I could help Hugo get started.'

After a couple of thoughtful moments, Jessie said, 'I might be able to help. My partner, Luis, has a little gallery not far from here.'

'Dance partner?'

'No, no. Life partner. I'm the dancing half; Luis is visual arts. One of these days I might agree to marry him. He's been asking for long enough. Come on! Let's go and see him.'

25

Luis was a small, dark man with a brooding intensity that lit up the dim interior of the gallery. The paintings on display were mostly seascapes, realistic pictures of breaking waves, fishing boats and rugged headlands.

It was obvious he was a very ardent admirer of Jessie, Sam thought with a knowing smile. He listened to Jessie's explanation intently, and then turned to Sam with a gracious welcome and a firm handshake.

'Please,' he said. 'The photographs. May I see them?'

She brought out the cards she had printed and also showed him the pictures on her phone. He studied them all, appearing interested. Then he asked if she had any actual paintings with her.

'In the car,' she said. 'Would you like to see them?'

'Please,' he said again.

'I'll give you a hand,' Jessie announced.

It took half an hour of quiet inspection, during which time Jessie made some coffee and regaled Sam with dance studio tales, before Luis came to say yes, he was very interested.

'I specialise in scenes of the Algarve,' he said. 'Just like these. Your friend is a fine artist, and I would like to show some of his work. I would like to meet him, as well, of course. Is that possible?'

Sam shook his hand again and with a big smile assured him that meeting Hugo certainly was possible.

'Is your friend Portuguese?' Luis asked. 'He must be, no?'

'I'm not sure,' she confessed. 'His parents were not, but all I really know is that Hugo has lived in Sao Bras all his life and seems to speak the language as well as any other native.'

'He is Portuguese,' Luis decided. 'He understands our landscape, and loves it.'

'Yes,' Sam said. 'You're right about that, I'm sure.'

* * *

There was a little more business to conduct but it didn't take long. Sam left it to Luis to decide on the prices of the paintings, and was happy to agree to the standard rate of commission the gallery charged. Then, with a lot of laughter and in a cloud of excitement, she departed. She couldn't wait to get back to Sao Bras to tell Hugo.

'Bring Hugo soon!' Luis called after her.

'I will! Don't worry about that.'

Bring Hugo? she thought happily. She wouldn't be able to keep him away!

* * *

In order to return Georgina's car, Sam drove straight to Casa Largo, thinking she would walk into Sao Bras to tell Hugo the good news. Unfortunately, she arrived in the midst of yet another argument between Georgina and Simon, and once again it seemed to be about money. As she headed for the office, she could hear them at it. Her spirits plummeted.

'There isn't any more!' she heard Georgina protest. 'We haven't got it.'

'There must be some!' Simon responded. 'It has to be paid.'

'I've told you. I haven't got it.'

'Ssh!' Sam demanded, bursting into the office. 'I could hear you both from the car park. People will be wondering what's going on.'

They turned to stare at her.

'Have you brought the car back?' Simon demanded.

'Yes, I have brought Georgina's car back,' Sam said coldly. 'Why?'

He turned away and picked up some papers from the desk.

'Georgina, what's going on?'

'Leave it, Sam. Just leave it. Please.'

Georgina got up and walked out of the office.

All this didn't augur well for the planned marriage, Sam thought. But maybe that wasn't such a bad thing. The marriage was something Sam certainly didn't want to see happen. Yet she wasn't at all happy.

'Simon, why on earth are you going on at Georgina about money all the time? What on earth is going on? You can see how upset she is. Even I can see that.'

'It's nothing to do with you,' he said curtly. 'Keep out of it.'

'Keep out of it?' she responded indignantly. 'Nothing to do with me? Everyone within a mile of Casa Largo can hear you arguing!'

If she hoped to draw him out into the open, it didn't work. Like Georgina before him, Simon got up and walked out, leaving her alone on the bridge.

Oh, fiddle! she thought despondently. I'm going to see Hugo.

* * *

Hugo, at least, was in a good mood. He listened, seemingly enchanted, as she told him about her day in Faro, and about Luis and his gallery.

'That's wonderful,' he said with a slow shake of his head, as if he could scarcely believe it. 'Goodness, Sam! You've done so well. I never expected anything like this.'

'Well, it's a start,' she cautioned. 'Nothing more. You've got your foot in the door. Hopefully, you'll get inside soon. But don't take anything for granted. Let's see what happens with Luis.

'Meanwhile,' she added, 'you've got to go down there and talk to him. Let him see what you look like, and hear what you have to say. He's a nice guy. I'm sure you'll like him. Jessie, his partner, too.'

'Next week,' Hugo said. 'I'll go to see him on Monday or Tuesday. Want to come?'

'Maybe. I'll have to see what Georgina says. Could we take your car?

I'm in danger of wearing your mum's car out.'

Hugo nodded and then said, 'We should have a glass of wine to celebrate.'

'What, now?'

'Why not?'

She smiled. 'I can't think of any reason why not. Let's do it.'

*   *   *

Soon afterwards Abby arrived, with Suzy in tow. The girls were friendly enough, but Sam knew she was receiving suspicious glances.

'Tell them, Hugo,' she said, anxious to have them know that her own presence was not cause for alarm. 'Tell them why I'm here.'

'Sam has just arranged for a gallery in Faro to hang some of my paintings,' Hugo said with a happy smile. 'Isn't that wonderful?'

'Oh, yes! Well done, Sam,' Suzy said immediately. 'That's great.'

'Yes, it is,' Abby said with less conviction. 'Come on! We're all going out.'

'Not me,' Sam said quickly. 'I'm on my way home. But enjoy yourselves.'

Hugo showed her to the door. 'Thanks again,' he said. 'What a day!'

She smiled. 'It is, isn't it? Enjoy yourself tonight, Hugo. I'll be in touch about the trip to see Luis.'

On the way home she found herself hoping Abby wasn't too bothered about her intervention in Hugo's life. She didn't need to be. Much as she liked Hugo, she was intent on doing nothing more than helping him realise his dream. Hopefully, Abby was grown-up enough to accept that. Too bad if she wasn't, which did seem a possibility. She would have to try to reassure her that she had no designs on Hugo.

Anyway, it really was a good day. She had done what she had set out to do for Hugo, and in that sense she was well pleased. She had done something worthwhile, and she knew that what she had done was appreciated. If Hugo was lucky, it would work out well for him and change his life. If not, nothing had been lost. They were giving it a go. That was the main thing.

26

Sam dug the phone out of her pocket.

'Sam? It's Jessie.'

'Oh, hello! How are you?'

'Working my socks off, and under-paid. You?'

Sam laughed. It was lovely to hear a voice from home, from near enough anyway. She wasn't homesick, or anything like it, but it was refreshing all the same. And Jessie, of course, had the power and the effervescence to reach parts other people couldn't.

'I shouldn't complain, because it keeps me in a job, but the work here never slows down. I'm losing weight and getting amazingly fit. I've got quite a good tan coming on, as well.'

'Oh, I have to keep out of the sun. With my complexion, all freckles and red hair, I'm a real indoor girl. Anyway,

I just rang to tell you Luis has sold one of Hugo's pictures.'

'Really? Oh, wow! He'll be over the moon. Which one?'

'I think it's the one of that big rock thing — wot's-its-name?'

Laughing, Sam said, 'That is a mountain, Jessie!'

'Like I said.'

'And it's called — hang on, let me think. It is called Rocha da Pena, I believe. Something like that. Anyway, that's wonderful news. What price did Luis get for it?'

'The price on the label.'

'It wasn't bargained down?'

'Huh? You don't know Luis. He would show you the door if you tried that with him. He doesn't run an auction, or a jumble sale, he'd say. The price he puts on a painting is what he believes it is worth — and that's that, come hail or shine.'

'I can believe that of him. He is a terribly serious man, isn't he?'

'Serious? You don't know the half of

it. But he's a good man, and his word is his bond.

'So I gathered, Jessie. You're lucky to have him — as he is to have you, of course!'

'He hasn't quite got me yet, pet. I haven't said yes, although I will eventually, I suppose.'

'Of course you will. You're made for each other. Anyway, I can't wait to pass on the good news to Hugo. He'll be thrilled. So thanks again for calling.'

'That's all right. Come down and see me again — soon.'

'I will. We both will, and we'll visit Luis again as well.'

⋆ ⋆ ⋆

Hugo was pleased, very much so. Thrilled, in fact. She caught him in his work clothes. Not a Picasso smock, as she had sometimes imagined, but in cut-off shorts, a liberally spattered tee-shirt and bare feet.

'Sam!' he exclaimed when he opened

the door. 'I didn't expect to see you this evening.'

'I'll go, then,' she said, pouting mischievously.

'Of course you won't. Come in. Have a drink.'

'Are you expecting Abby?'

'What — dressed like this?' he said, laughing.

'No, I don't suppose you are,' she said, thinking of how glamorous both Abby and Suzy always looked.

'I've brought good news,' she said, getting straight to the point. 'Jessie rang earlier to tell me. Luis has sold one of your paintings. The one of Rocha da Pena. Is that right?'

Hugo gaped at her while he digested the news.

'That's great!' he managed eventually. 'Wonderful. Incredible.'

'Isn't it? I knew you'd be pleased.'

'We should go out and celebrate,' he said, 'but I need a shower and clean clothes, and . . . '

'Not tonight, Hugo. I just came over

to tell you the news. I wanted to see your face when I told you.'

'You can't stay?'

She shook her head. 'Sorry. I can't,' she lied. 'Things to do back at the ranch.'

Hugo looked disappointed, which almost made her self-sacrifice worthwhile. There was nothing she would have liked more than to stay a while, but she wasn't going to get in the way of Hugo and Abby. The last thing she wanted was to cause friction there. More friction, she qualified, suspecting that Abby was already suspicious and on guard.

* * *

On the way back to Casa Largo, she felt so happy that she had been able to help Hugo. She thought she had probably done as much as she could for the moment. It was down to him now, him and Luis. Knowing Hugo as she did, and knowing his aspirations, she was

234

sure he would go from strength to strength.

All she had to do now, she thought with a grimace, was sort out Simon, and stop Georgina making the mistake of her life. Then her conscience would be clear. She really would have done everything she could for them all. Maybe then it would be time to leave.

That was a thought that troubled her for a moment. Where had it come from? Why would she even think that? She liked it here. Why should she leave? Well, Hugo, for one thing. He was meant for Abby, it seemed. She would wish them both well for the future, but she wasn't going to hang around to have her disappointment confirmed.

Having said all that, leaving might well be some time off yet. She couldn't go before she settled Simon's hash, and it frustrated her that she had made no real progress there. She still didn't have enough to take to Georgina without being sent packing for her troubles. In fact, she had next to nothing. Just suspicions and circumstantial evidence, and the undeniable fact that Simon had been downright unpleasant in those frequent arguments about money. She really did have to get a move on.

One good thing was that she hadn't heard any more talk of an imminent wedding. Presumably financial realities had dampened passion down, which wasn't a bad thing from her point of view. The more the couple's plans were delayed the better. A firm date of 'Never' would suit her even more.

★　★　★

Such thoughts vanished when she got back to Casa Largo. There, she found poor Georgina sitting alone on the terrace in tears. She grimaced and thought: Oh, dear! What on earth has that terrible man done now?

27

'What is it?' Sam cried, rushing over to Georgina. 'What's happened?'

'Nothing,' Georgina said, covering her face with her hands for a moment. 'Nothing at all.'

Sam stood and studied her. Something was wrong. She could see that. She put her arms around Georgina and gave her a hug. Then she sat down on one of the spare wicker chairs around the table.

'I'm so sorry,' Georgina said, straightening up and reaching for a tissue. 'I thought I was alone.'

'Is Simon here?'

Georgina shook her head. 'He's gone now.'

I just bet he has! Sam thought angrily. He's done his damage and left. It was terrible he could get away with it. A way had to be found of stopping him.

'Can I get you some lemonade from the fridge?' Sam asked.

'Thank you. That would be lovely.'

Everything seemed in order in the kitchen. There were dishes to be washed, but nothing had been broken. Whatever had gone on, the assault had been more psychological than physical. Not that that made it any better.

By the time she returned with two glasses of lemonade, Georgina had managed to pull herself together.

'I've just been over to see Hugo,' Sam said. 'The gallery in Faro phoned me to say they had sold one of his paintings.'

'Oh?' Georgina looked at her with interest. 'That's good, isn't it?'

'It's wonderful! Hugo is thrilled about it.'

'I'll bet.' Georgina looked at her speculatively. 'You've been helping him, haven't you? He has a lot to thank you for.'

Sam shrugged. 'I haven't done much, but I found a nice Geordie woman in Faro whose partner runs an art gallery.

They agreed to exhibit some of his paintings. Now this!' she added happily.

'You've done a lot more for him than I ever have. And I know how pleased and grateful he is.'

'Nonsense, Georgina! You're his mother. No-one can ever do more than your mother. All I did was think about how he could get a start with selling his paintings, and making a living from them. That didn't take long.'

'No, no!' Georgina said sharply. 'Once again you're underestimating your own contribution, Sam, just as you do here. I don't know where I would have been if you hadn't come to help.'

'You would have been perfectly all right, Georgina. I know that. Anyway, I gather Hugo told you what I've been doing?'

'Some of it. I must admit I was surprised.'

'Well, I just wanted to help. Randolph told me Hugo painted, but nothing more. Then, when I saw some of his pictures I thought they were wonderful.'

'Did you really?'

Sam nodded vigorously. 'Extraordinary, really. I mean, I haven't seen much of the Algarve — we've been too busy here — but as soon as I saw Hugo's paintings I felt that he had got it right. He had captured the essence of the region. And I just wanted to help him with the marketing.'

'It's funny,' Georgina said thoughtfully. 'I never thought his paintings would be any good.'

'Well, I don't know how good they are in a formal sense. I'm not qualified to judge. But I can't see that that matters. I like them very much indeed — and I like Hugo.'

Georgina smiled. 'I just thought he was making a fuss about painting because he wanted to get out of doing any work here.'

'Oh, Georgina! What a thing to say.'

'Well, Randolph thought the same

thing, and he's an artist.'

'Randolph? What did he say?'

She thought back to how disparaging he had been when he spoke to her about Hugo's work.

Georgina shrugged. 'He just gave me the impression that they weren't up to much. If Hugo had gone to art school, he said, then maybe he would have learned how to paint properly. Randolph knows about these things. I don't.'

'I'm not at all sure he does know,' Sam said firmly. 'Randolph seems to have a fixed idea of what an artist, and art, is, but as I told Hugo that's just his personal opinion. I even wonder if he might not be just a little bit jealous.'

'Randolph?' Georgina said quickly. 'Oh, I hardly think so. He's a fine old gentleman, and a professional artist — if you can say that.'

'Yes,' Sam said, 'but how many paintings has he sold lately?'

'None, I don't think. He . . . '

'Well, Hugo has sold one!'

Almost reluctantly, Georgina began to smile, and then to laugh.

'You're good for me, Sam,' she said with a chuckle. 'I do like having you here!'

'That's all very well,' Sam said with a grin, 'but now tell me what on earth was going on this evening, before I arrived. Simon was here, you said. What happened to upset you so much?'

'Oh, the same old thing.'

'What? Money?'

Georgina nodded. 'I'm afraid our finances are not what they should be, and they're certainly not what I hoped they would be at this point.'

'Why not? What's the problem?'

Perhaps now, Sam was thinking, she will tell me what Simon has been up to. Then we can try to straighten things out, and change her mind about Simon.

'It's just the general economy, the recession, or whatever it is they call it. Takings have gone down and down these last few years. I've been scratching and saving, here and there. Simon arrived this evening with a big bill that needs paying, and suddenly it was all too much.

'I'm sorry,' Georgina added. 'It's just that sometimes . . .'

'I know. I understand. Life isn't easy at times. I thought I had a good job and could see my way ahead, and then suddenly I was redundant and things became frightening. You don't have to explain, Georgina.'

'It will get better,' Georgina said softly.

Sam wondered if she meant when she and Simon were married, which was a frightening prospect in itself.

'The wedding . . . ?' she began.

'We've postponed it for now,' Georgina said quickly.

Phew! No need to bring that up yet then, Sam thought with relief.

'But I think that's just made things worse,' Georgina added dispiritedly.

'About Simon,' Sam began tactfully. 'Do you honestly think he is the right person . . .'

'For me?' Georgina said sharply. 'Of course he is! Simon is wonderful. I couldn't be without him.'

'I didn't mean that,' Sam said, floundering desperately as she tried to get back to safe ground. 'I meant more in the . . . well, in the financial sense.'

'Oh, I see. Well, it's the same answer. Simon is wonderful there, too. He squeezes the last drops out of the lemon even when there seems to be nothing left in it. Time and again, he does it.'

Yes, I can see that, Sam thought wearily. Would she ever be able to tell Georgina what was really on her mind?

'Come on, Sam. We've got a long day tomorrow. Better get ourselves away to bed before the madding crowds arrive.'

28

Over the next few weeks, Hugo sold a few more of his pictures. Or, rather, Luis did. Luis said there was always an influx of wealthy tourists as the season marched on, some of them with boats in the marina, and quite a few of them with investment as well as souvenirs in mind. On both counts, Hugo's paintings were attractive. So they sold. Hugo was pleased; Luis was pleased. And so were Sam and Jessie.

'You're going to have to paint faster,' Jessie told him on one of the visits Hugo and Sam made to the gallery in Faro. 'You're in danger of holding Luis up!'

Luis tut-tutted in the background. He was a serious man, passionate about art as well as about Jessie. He didn't approve of such levity. Well, not during working hours. He was different when they were over. Jessie was embarrassingly frank about that. It made Sam glad she had Hugo for company.

On the drive back to Sao Bras, she said, 'This road is becoming very familiar, isn't it?'

Hugo glanced sideways at her and said with a smile, 'It's a pity we can't send them my paintings by email? Is that what you're thinking?'

'No, not at all.' Sam laughed happily. 'I enjoy getting away from Casa Largo from time to time. Our trips to Faro are very enjoyable. For you, too, I think?'

He seemed comically dubious.

'Hugo, you can't paint all the time. You have to have a life, as well!'

He laughed at that.

She turned away to watch the fields flashing past, the fields of bare earth and scrubland, and then those where irrigation had produced vivid green grassland. How lucky the sheep with grass to eat were, she thought. Most of the sheep she had seen seemed to subsist on sticks and twigs, and whatever else they could find that nothing and nobody else wanted.

'That farm you are painting, Hugo. Where is it?'

'The other side of the village of Alportel.'

She had seen his work in progress, a picture of somewhere more like a botanic garden than a farm. Figs and palm trees, oranges and bananas. Vegetable beds full of wonderful onions and peppers. Climbing beans up at a height. Picturesque.

'You should paint somewhere . . . '

'I'm going to,' he said quickly, cutting her off.

'You're . . . ?'

'A friend of mine has a place down here. Not a hill farm. Just goats and chickens, and bare ground in summer. Not everywhere is the same.'

She thought for a moment and then said, 'How did you know what I was going to say?'

Hugo just shrugged.

'You did, didn't you?'

He smiled now.

She smiled back. It was often like that. He knew, and she knew. They pulled together. That was how it was, how it had become.

★ ★ ★

Abby was waiting in her car outside Hugo's flat, her face thunderous. Sam winced inwardly when she saw her. She guessed it wasn't going to be good.

'Hello, Abby!' she said brightly.

'Hello.'

Sam would have said more but Abby was focused on Hugo, rather than her.

'Where have you been, Hugo? I've been waiting half an hour.'

Hugo looked puzzled. 'Have you?' He smiled, trying to reassure her, and said, 'Abby, I did tell you Sam and I were visiting the gallery in Faro today. We've just got back.'

Abby was undeflected. 'We were supposed to be joining Suzy and some of the others this evening. Look at the time!'

'Oh? Did I know about that? I don't remember you saying . . . '

'You might have guessed, Hugo! You know I like to go out in the evening. How could I go alone?'

Sam decided to risk intervening. 'Abby, this was quite an important visit today. Hugo had to talk to the owner of the gallery, in order to . . . '

'Important? Not to me it wasn't. Anyway, Sam, keep out of it, if you don't mind. This is between me and Hugo.'

'I think you're being a little unfair,' Sam said firmly, 'especially if Hugo didn't know something had been arranged, and considering that he had told you what he was intending to do.'

Abby turned her back on her, and let fly at Hugo. 'You think more of your stupid paintings than you do of me!'

Hugo shrugged. 'They are what I do, Abby. You knew that when we met. You said then that you appreciated it, that you liked art.'

'Not every day! Well, I've had enough. That's it. I don't want anything more to do with you, or your paintings. It's over. Goodbye! That's all I wanted to tell you.'

With that, Abby stormed off to her car.

'I hope she'll be safe to drive,' Hugo said, not sounding terribly worried.

'I wouldn't try to stop her, if I were you,' Sam advised.

'No,' he agreed. 'That would probably be a mistake. Come on! Let's go inside and have a coffee or a glass of wine, or something. We have a lot to celebrate.'

Sam followed Hugo indoors, feeling more than a little guilty about the outburst she had just witnessed. Was it down to her? Perhaps it was. Not intentionally, but even so she couldn't deny her role in things. Hugo wouldn't have gone to Faro if it hadn't been for her.

In the kitchen Hugo put on the kettle. Then they stood and waited, and looked at each other.

'I'm so sorry, Hugo.'

'For what?'

'Well, I feel partly responsible. Abby probably doesn't realise she has nothing to be jealous about. Our trip to Faro was about your paintings, nothing else. I don't know what else she thinks happened, but I can imagine.'

He shook his head. 'Abby knows all that. There's nothing for you to worry about.'

'Well, I'm sorry for you, too. Maybe you can patch it up? Go and see her. Explain. I'm sure she'll understand.'

'Forget it, Sam.'

The kettle shrieked. He turned his attention to making two mugs of coffee.

'Besides,' he said, turning to stare at her, 'it wasn't only about the paintings, was it? Be honest with me.'

She stared back, and found herself shaking her head. 'No,' she said reluctantly. 'It wasn't.'

'It wasn't for me either,' he said softly, taking her in his arms.

She closed her eyes and let him kiss her, and didn't even think about how long she had waited for him to do that.

★ ★ ★

'What about Abby?' Sam whispered later.

Hugo shrugged.

'Is it really over?'

'Of course it is. You heard her. It was never serious anyway, for either of us. We just did things together, that's all. Mostly we went to parties together, parties I didn't like with people I couldn't stand.'

'Are you sure?' Sam asked, hardly daring to believe her ears.

'Positive. I'd wanted to end it for a long time, but Abby seemed happy with the arrangement. So I just let it go on. I'm glad she took the initiative.

'Anyway,' he added, 'it won't take her

long to find someone else to go to parties with. There'll soon be a queue of applicants around the block.'

'You're so cynical!' Sam protested, laughing despite herself.

'Who, me?'

'Yes, you!'

She knew he was right, though, right about everything he had said. Hugo and Abby never had seemed suited to each other. So it was probably just as well Abby had put an end to it. They could both move on now.

All the same, it was too soon, too much like opportunism, for her to be stepping into the breach like this.

'I must go,' she said, disentangling herself.

'Must you?' Hugo asked wistfully.

'I must,' she said, more firmly. 'Let's give ourselves a little time and space, and then see how we feel.'

'Sure.' He smiled and kissed her on the forehead. 'You're probably right.'

'Besides,' she added, forgetting she had told him nothing about her secret mission, 'I've still got to deal with Simon.'

'Oh, yes!' Hugo said with a groan. 'I certainly won't listen to him again.'

*   *   *

On the way back to Casa Largo, she wondered what on earth he had meant by that statement. Then she remembered he had told her once that Simon had introduced him to Abby. Quite right! she thought with a grin. Don't listen to him again.

29

Things had changed. Sam didn't want to think about it too much, but things had changed between Hugo and herself. There was no mistaking it. They had even admitted it to each other. But she wasn't going to go wild. She was going to take her time, and make sure Hugo did too. No rushing into things this time. All the same, she thought with a delicious shiver, things had changed.

Meanwhile, Hugo had his painting and she had the Simon problem to deal with. They both had plenty to do. Now, especially now, she would redouble her efforts to free Casa Largo of Simon. That was her mission.

★ ★ ★

From the little café across the street from the Bliss building, a day or two later, she was watching when a young woman emerged from the Bliss office itself. The woman stumbled slightly on the steps and paused to re-balance herself, and to dab at her eyes with a tissue. She seemed to be in shock, scarcely able to put one foot in front of the other.

Shocked herself, and holding her breath, Sam gasped and leant forward, staring with horror. What on earth had happened?

It was the first time she had seen anyone but Simon go in or come out of that office. She had begun to think it would never happen. Now this!

The woman was upset. She stood there, holding on to the wall, alternately dabbing at her eyes and straightening herself up, seemingly undecided as to what to do next.

Simon! Sam thought angrily. What has he done now?

Without thinking any further, she pushed her chair back with a screech, got up and left the café. She crossed the road quickly and with concern approached the woman.

'What's wrong?' she asked softly. 'Do you need help?'

The woman glanced at her and shook her head. Then she lowered her eyes. She looked as if something absolutely appalling had happened to her.

She was perhaps thirty-ish, slender and blonde, though not a natural blonde. More like expensive-hair-do blonde. She was well dressed in a flowing summer dress in a floral pattern.

'Are you sure?' Sam pressed urgently. 'You don't seem well. Do you feel faint? Has something happened?'

The woman looked up at her appraisingly. 'Do you speak English?' she asked, as if she had scarcely heard a word Sam had said.

Sam smiled reassuringly and nodded. 'Would you like to sit down somewhere and have a coffee, while you recover?' she asked. 'There's a little café across the street. I was in there when I saw you stumble on the steps. I thought you needed help.'

'Help?' the woman said. 'No, I don't need help. Not in that sense. I'm . . . I'm all right, I suppose.'

'I don't think you are,' Sam said firmly. 'You look as if you have had a terrible shock. You need to sit down for a few minutes, and rest. Come on! Let me buy you a coffee.'

They got across the street safely and into the café, where they sat down at a table well away from the window.

'Would you like coffee?' Sam asked. 'Or do you prefer something else? Tea, perhaps? A cold drink?'

'Coffee would be nice. Thank you.'

Sam went up to the counter to place her order.

When she returned, the woman straightened herself up and made an effort. 'You're very kind,' she said. 'Thank you. You're right. I have had a shock. I didn't know what to do about it. I still don't.'

Sam shrugged and smiled reassuringly. 'We all need help from time to time. Did you hurt your ankle when you stumbled on the steps?'

'No, not my ankle.'

'Your knee, then?'

The woman shook her head.

Their coffee came, brought by the proprietor who was obviously very curious about what was going on.

'This lady slipped on some steps,' Sam told him quickly. 'She had a shock.'

He rolled his eyes upwards and withdrew. Not his business.

'I saw you come out of the Bliss office,' Sam said, 'and I guessed you had had a bad experience there.'

The woman pulled a face. 'It wasn't exactly blissful,' she admitted with a wan smile.

At least she could joke about it, Sam thought. That was a good sign. She was recovering.

'Oh, dear. Did he want money, more money?'

'No, he gave me my money back. He apologised for what had happened, and said it was just one of those things, unfortunately.'

'I'll bet he did!' Sam said grimly. 'But he didn't threaten you or demand more money?'

The woman just looked at her, seemingly puzzled by the question. 'What do you mean? Who do you mean, I should say?'

'Simon Kendrew, of course, the man you borrowed the money from in the first place. If he didn't threaten you, you were very lucky.'

She paused for thought, puzzled, and added, 'But what did you mean when you said he gave you your money back? From a previous instalment, you mean?'

The woman came to life, as if from hibernation, and was suddenly very animated. 'It was nothing like that,' she said heatedly. 'Nothing at all!'

'Oh?'

The woman shook her head. 'Mr Kendrew was lovely. He apologised and said he was very sad about what had happened. Like I said, he even gave me my subscription back. He couldn't have been nicer.'

Sam spent a few moments uneasily working her way around that. Subscription? That didn't sound right. It didn't sound like the Simon Kendrew she knew either.

'But you did borrow money from him?' she said less confidently.

'No, of course not!' The woman shook her head vigorously. 'If I needed money, which I don't, I would have gone to the bank — or to my ex-husband. Whatever gave you that idea?'

Sam shrugged and blew out her cheeks in her confusion. 'I thought that was what Bliss does — lend people money?'

The woman began to smile, an expression Sam had not expected to see on that hitherto sad face. She also shook her head.

'What?' Sam said defensively.

'It's nothing like that,' the woman said with a big smile now. 'Bliss is an online dating agency!'

'A dating agency?'

The woman nodded. And added, 'It's mostly for expats, like me.'

Sam stared, incredulous, and rendered speechless for the moment.

'Bliss?' she said eventually. 'It's not a money business?'

'*Bliss*,' the woman said slowly, and emphatically. 'Get it now?'

And now she did: *Bliss*.

She groaned and sighed, both at the same time. How could she ever have thought it was anything other than what it was, than what its name suggested?'

'The man I was so upset about,' the woman continued, 'wasn't Mr Kendrew. It was Jeremy, this man I met through the agency. He behaved very badly to me. So I came here to let them know, and to work out what to do about it.

'It's a bit of a leap in the dark,' she confided, 'when you go on a blind date with someone an agency put you in touch with. They do the best they can, but it doesn't always work out well. It can't be expected to, can it?'

Sam shook her head in tacit agreement.

'And Simon Kendrew gave you your money back?' she said faintly. 'Your subscription, you said?'

The woman — who had not long ago been so distressed — nodded and said, 'Shall we have another coffee?'

30

They had a second coffee, Sam and the woman whose name she never did learn, and then they parted, with mutual assurances that they would get together again sometime. Quite how they would do that didn't figure in the conversation.

Not in this life! Sam swore to herself as she walked away from the café, and from the woman and the Bliss building. I'm never doing that again — any of it! What a humiliation.

She had struggled for many minutes to come to terms with the absolute enormity of her mistake, and her consequent embarrassment. It had been a slow process, one to make her cringe.

It had taken her a while to accept that Simon Kendrew was neither a money launderer nor a loan shark, and quite possibly not a criminal of any description. She failed even to address the question of whether she still believed he was operating under a false identity. She had cringed enough!

The only good thing to have come out of it, she thought ruefully, clutching desperately at straws, was that the woman she had tried to help had been a lot happier by the time they parted. She had seemed in wonderful spirits by the end, quite recovered from her earlier desperate straits. Happy, even. Sam's initial incomprehension and then embarrassment had both contributed hugely to her recovery.

Well, that's it, Sam thought with a grim expression. Now I'm going to find out what's really been going on at Casa Largo. I'm not going to be put off or inhibited any more. I've paid my dues. I'm entitled. And if they don't like it, they can jolly well fire me! See if I care.

★ ★ ★

She found Georgina sitting disconsolately in the office back at Casa Largo, staring unproductively at a blank wall. Furious, humiliated and uninhibited, Sam waded straight in.

'Georgina, I've just about had enough! What on earth is going on around here?'

'Sam! Hello, dear. Where have you been?'

'Downtown, staking out the Bliss building.'

Georgina peered at her as if she thought she wasn't quite right in the head.

'Please don't look at me like that, Georgina!'

'Well, dear, I don't . . . '

'It's a long story, and I'm not even sure if I will ever tell you the whole of it. What I want to know is what's going on here, before I make any more mistakes. What is Simon up to with his dating agency, for a start?'

'Oh, that.'

'Yes, that. If I'd known earlier, it might have stopped me making a fool of myself. I thought he was money laundering or running a loan sharking business. Nobody told me it was a dating agency!'

Georgina stared, bewildered. Then she gathered herself together and reluctantly began to address the question.

'I don't really know what you're talking about, Sam, but perhaps this is a good time to explain one or two things I've been keeping from you. I didn't want to spoil your time here with us by having you worry about things that were nothing to do with you.' Georgina peered at her uncertainly and added, 'I gather things are different now?'

'They certainly are! I want you to tell me before I embarrass myself any further.'

'Well, as you already know, Casa Largo's finances are a bit shaky at the moment. We will turn things around when the economy improves. I'm sure of that. But in the meantime, we are where we are. Not in a good place.'

'You've told me all that before, Georgina.'

'Have I really? Well, yes. Perhaps I have.'

Sam flopped down in a chair and waited for Georgina to get on with it. Her agitation was beginning to calm down. She was beginning to think that perhaps she might survive this near-death experience after all.

'To cut a long story short,' Georgina said, 'Simon and I put our heads together to think about what we could do to improve the situation. We discussed many possibilities before Simon came up with the idea of an online dating agency for expats living in the region.

'He's good with computers, IT stuff, and it seemed an excellent idea. We could generate a new business, and extra revenue, to help get the Casa Largo business out of its problems.'

'And out of that, Bliss was born?'

'Exactly.' Georgina smiled. 'It's a

lovely name for it, isn't it?'

Sam smiled, too, and she wondered ruefully how she could ever have thought it was about anything to do with money.

There had been so many clues, if only she had bothered to consider them, and put them together. First, Hugo had said he and Abby had got together through Simon, and then Suzy had confirmed it. How else could it ever have happened? They were not people who moved in the same circles, or who had the same interests. They were not even the same age.

Then Esmeralda had virtually told her that Mr Kendrew and Mr Bliss were the same person. She should have worked out what that meant.

And the café proprietor had said Bliss was something to do with computers. Oh, there were other clues too! The way, for example, that no customers ever went through the door. If only she had had the wit to put all that together, she would have come to a different conclusion.

'I suppose Simon was always demanding money from you to pay bills, was he?'

Georgina nodded. 'The business account is in my name only. He needed me to forward the money.'

Sam sighed wearily. 'And there I was, thinking he was blackmailing you, or something.'

'Oh, Sam!' Georgina laughed. 'Simon? How could you think that?'

Sam shook her head. She didn't know now. 'Just one of my many mistakes,' she admitted.

'Anyway, Simon got the agency up and running, and it's been a great help. We're not exactly rolling in cash, but we're no longer teetering on the edge of bankruptcy either. Our slide towards disaster has been slowed,' Georgina added wryly, 'even if it hasn't altogether stopped.'

'So it's been a good thing to do, hasn't it?'

'It's certainly helped financially. But

there's been a downside, too. Lemonade?' Georgina asked, breaking off to
reach for a jug on the table.

'Yes, please. I've done so much
talking today that I need some sort of
lubricant. Is lemonade good for the
brain, too?'

'I wouldn't be surprised.'

Georgina poured Sam a glass, and
another for herself. 'Now, where was I?'

'There's a downside to Bliss, you
said.'

'Oh, yes. Poor Simon is worn out. He
has been working night and day, and
has ended up living in town in a flat he
borrowed from a friend who is away for
a few months. So I hardly ever seem to
see him these days.

'When he is here, he's too exhausted
to do much. The office work he's
supposed to do piles up, and bills don't
get paid. Sometimes he's desperate to
pay a bill but there's nothing left in the
bank account. So we're both arguing
and snapping at each other, and at
Hugo as well.'

'I've heard some of that,' Sam admitted. 'It's not good, is it?'

Georgina shook her head. 'Meanwhile, the financial slide downhill has slowed but it continues. If Simon could only spend more time working at Bliss we could be pulling clear of the rocks, but he can't. He needs to do things here, too, things that I can't manage. I don't know what's going to happen to us all, if we go on like this.'

Georgina lapsed into a brooding silence. Sam let her be, while she did some thinking. What if . . . ?

She wasn't sure. She needed to think it through a bit more. There were implications, and there would be consequences. Then Esmeralda came to mind. She could help. So maybe it would be possible.

'Georgina, I want to suggest something for you to consider. It might not be acceptable, but if you agree it might help.'

'What's that?'

'How would it be if I took over the

running of the office, here at Casa Largo? I'm sure I would still have plenty of time to continue with most of what I do already, and that would leave Simon free to focus on Bliss.

'He could generate more revenue that way — and at the same time get more sleep, and see more of you. We could ask Esmeralda to come in a bit more often with the cleaning, if needs be. What do you think?'

'You, Sam?' Georgina looked at her with astonishment. 'You think you could run the office?'

'Office work is what I've done all my working life, as I told you once before.'

'It isn't just filing bits of paper and taking cheques to the bank, you know,' Georgina said tartly. 'Effectively, it's running the commercial side of the business.'

'Looking after the website, advertising, accounts, writing letters and emails, dealing with phone calls, talking to suppliers?'

'Well, yes.'

'I can do that, and more.'

Georgina stared at her thoughtfully. 'Can you really?'

Sam nodded. Then she smiled. 'I was the office manager at MacDonald & Flanagan, my last job. If you want a reference, my old boss will happily give you a good one, I'm sure.'

'Well,' Georgina said. 'I don't know what to say. You've given me a lot to think about. What a wonderfully interesting proposal. Are you sure about this?'

'Of course I am! I love it here, and I want to help save Casa Largo. This is my big adventure, my Casa Largo adventure! When I write my memoirs, I shall write about it.'

Georgina laughed. 'And what a story that will be. Well, bless you, my dear! I think you've come up with the solution to our problems.'

She looked up then, past Sam, and said, 'You can come in now, Hugo! No need to stand out there. Come and hear what Sam is proposing.'

Sam spun round. 'Hugo! I didn't know you were there. How long . . . ?'

'All the time,' he said cheerfully. 'I heard everything.'

He came across the room, wrapped his arms around Sam and said to Georgina, 'This person is going to be the saviour of us all.'

Georgina stared for a moment and then, smiling, said, 'I think you're right, Hugo. We're lucky to have found her.'

'Aren't we just?'

Georgina nodded, as if to herself, and added, 'So that's all right, as well. I was beginning to think nothing would ever happen between you two.'

'It is,' Hugo agreed. 'At least, I think it is,' he added, looking at Sam.

'Of course it is!' she assured him, laughing happily. 'We both know that, don't we?'

'We've known it all along. We just didn't want to admit it.'

'Don't mind me,' Georgina said. 'Give her a kiss!'

So he did.

'What's all right?' a new voice demanded.

Sam spun round again, this time to see Simon standing in the entrance, a big smile on his face.

'Come in, come in!' Georgina said excitedly. 'We have things to tell you, darling! Lots of things.'

Simon came in and sat down, and listened to what Georgina had to say. It made him smile even more.

'Good!' he said when she was finished. 'I was afraid I was going to be loaded with even more work, but it's less. Thank you, Sam. That's an excellent proposal.'

He eyed her shrewdly then and added, 'You and I haven't always seen eye to eye, Sam, but . . . '

'Misunderstandings,' she said, shrugging it off. 'I just didn't know what was going on, and invented my own explanations. I got a lot of things very wrong.'

'That was our fault. We didn't want you worrying about our problems —

but you did anyway!'

He chuckled and shook his head. 'All I really wanted to say was that now we're all on the same team, I'm very glad you're here. We need you. I can see Hugo does, too,' he added with a grin.

'Oh, yes!' Hugo admitted, giving her a hug. 'If she never sells another of my paintings, I still want her to stay.'

Sam gave him a grateful smile, and a hug, and said, 'If you've all finished being nice to me, I've got work to do!'

THE END

MEET ME AT MIDNIGHT

Gael Morrison

Nate Robbins needs the money bequeathed to him by his eccentric uncle — but in order to get it he must remarry before his thirtieth birthday, three weeks away. Deserted by her husband, Samantha Feldon is determined not to marry again unless she's sure the love she finds is true. So when her boss — Nate Robbins — offers her the job of 'wife', she refuses, but agrees to help him find someone suitable. Accompanying him on a Caribbean cruise, Sam finds him the perfect woman — realizing too late she loves Nate herself . . .

LOOKING FOR LAURIE

Beth James

On finding a dead body in her flat, Laurie Kendal fights her instinct to scream, and instead races to the nearest police station. About to embark upon a cycling holiday, DI Tom Jessop attends the scene, only to find . . . nothing! The body has inexplicably disappeared, and so he dismisses Laurie's story as rubbish. But there is something intriguing about Laurie — she is beautifully eccentric, yet vulnerable too, and earnest in her insistence that her story is true. So before starting his holiday, Tom has one more check on her flat . . .

A CHRISTMAS ENGAGEMENT

Jill Barry

Adjusting to life without her late husband, Molly Reid is determined to make the most of a holiday to Madeira. As the dreamlike days of surf and sun pass, a friendship with her tour guide Michael develops and grows, though she wonders whether his attention and care are just part of his job. Back in Wales, meanwhile, Molly's daughter and son-in-law are hatching a surprise family reunion over Christmas — and it looks like the family could be about to gain some new members . . .